Dear Reader,

We have exciting news! Starting in January, the Harlequin Blaze books you know and love will be getting a brand-new look. And it's *hot!* Turn to the back of this book for a sneak peek....

But don't worry—nothing else about the Blaze books has changed. You'll still find those unforgettable love stories with intrepid heroines, hot, hunky heroes and a double dose of sizzle!

So be sure to check out our new supersexy covers. You'll find these newly packaged Blaze editions on the shelves December 18th, 2012, wherever you buy your books.

In the meantime, check out this month's red-hot reads.

LET IT SNOW by Leslie Kelly and Jennifer LaBrecque
(A Blazing Bedtime Stories Holiday Edition)

HIS FIRST NOELLE by Rhonda Nelson
(Men Out of Uniform)

ON A SNOWY CHRISTMAS NIGHT by Debbi Rawlins
(Made in Montana)

NICE & NAUGHTY by Tawny Weber

ALL I WANT FOR CHRISTMAS
by Lori Wilde, Kathleen O'Reilly and Candace Havens
(A Sizzling Yuletide Anthology)

HERS FOR THE HOLIDAYS by Samantha Hunter
(The Berringers)

Happy holidays!

Brenda Chin
Senior Editor
Harlequin Blaze

Rhonda Nelson

HIS FIRST NOELLE

HARLEQUIN®

entertain, enrich, inspire™

Recycling programs
for this product may
not exist in your area.

ISBN-13: 978-0-373-79728-8

HIS FIRST NOELLE

www.Harlequin.com

Printed in U.S.A.

ABOUT THE AUTHOR

A Waldenbooks bestselling author, two-time RITA®
Award nominee, *RT Book Reviews* Reviewers' Choice
nominee and National Readers' Choice Award winner
Rhonda Nelson writes hot romantic comedy for the Harlequin Blaze line and other Harlequin Books imprints.
With more than thirty-five published books to her
credit, she's thrilled with her career and enjoys dream-
ing up her characters and manipulating the worlds they
live in. She and her family make their chaotic but happy
home in a small town in northern Alabama. She loves
to hear from her readers, so be sure to check her out at
www.readRhondaNelson.com, follow her on Twitter
@RhondaRNelson and like her on Facebook.

Books by Rhonda Nelson

For all of our military and their families, most especially those who will spend the holidays apart. My heartfelt thanks for your service.

Prologue

MILITARY SNIPER JUDD WILLINGHAM ignored the sweat sliding into his eyes and the nausea climbing the back of his throat and snugged his finger tight against the trigger. His heart pounded so hard he could hear it thundering in his ears and the metallic taste of panic clung to his dry tongue. He didn't move—he'd learned to be perfectly still—his body flat against the sandy ground, his weapon positioned perfectly on the tripod.

"In range, clear shot," his spotter, Lewis Masterson said, his disembodied voice coming through the headset.

He knew, dammit. He *knew*. And yet…

"Captain?"

"I see, Lewis," he said, his voice raspy through his tightened throat.

His First Noelle

Clear target, in range, perfect shot. A so-called humane kill. The miserable sonofabitch lined up in his crosshairs had been strapping bombs onto terrified children and then sending them into the marketplace before remote detonating. The man deserved to die, if you asked him, and up until a month ago Judd hadn't minded meting out justice, had proudly embraced his Angel of Death moniker.

So why in the name of all that was holy couldn't he pull the godforsaken trigger? Why couldn't he do what he'd been trained to do? What he knew how to do best? Better than anybody, he'd been told. What he'd been doing for Uncle Sam for the past five years? Why the sudden attack of nerves, of conscience?

Why did he want to be anywhere but here, doing anything but this?

"Captain, you gonna take the shot?" Lewis prodded again, a hint of galling uncertainty in his voice.

He wanted to, dammit. It was his duty, his job, his purpose. He forcibly swallowed back the bile in his throat, dry heaved and readied himself once more. His target hadn't moved. *He could do this,* Judd told himself. *Had* to do this. He released a breath, narrowed his gaze, and then put his finger determinedly against the trigger and…

"He's moving, Angel! He's moving!" Lewis exclaimed. "Take the shot! Take him out!"

Judd hesitated.

Lewis didn't.

Captain Judd Willingham hung his head in as much shame as relief, swore softly under his breath and knew beyond a shadow of a doubt that his career in the military was officially over.

1

Six months later...

DRESSED IN A courier's uniform, newly minted security agent Judd Willingham made the short walk up the cracked sidewalk to the small front porch of the nondescript brick house. Twinkling Christmas lights with more burnt-out bulbs than working ones sagged from the eaves and a sad-looking wreath hung from a door in desperate need of a fresh coat of paint. Dead weeds, their crispy skeletons all that remained from a robust summer, pushed up between the evergreen shrubs, crowding the flower beds on either side of the entrance, and a rusty mailbox hung drunkenly from a lone nail which was dangerously close to slipping from the mortar. Judd grimaced.

This was the safe house? Really?

Granted he hadn't expected a mansion—the little town of Mossy Ridge, Mississippi, could barely afford its five-man police force, let alone a state-of-the-art safe house—but surely something a little more sound could have been made available. Considering this was the third time his target, Noelle Montgomery, had been evacuated due to another failed attempt on her life, no doubt their choices were dwindling.

Honestly, when he'd been briefed on his first assignment for Ranger Security, Judd had expected something a little less grave than protecting a key witness to a murder trial. After all, Jeb, his twin brother—older by two minutes and his exact mirror opposite—had merely had to find a jewel thief burgling a high-end retirement community. No life-or-death situation there. In fact, other than potentially getting run over by a motorized scooter, he hadn't been in any danger at all. At least physically, anyway. Judd inwardly grinned. His heart was another matter altogether. Much to their equal astonishment, Jeb had found himself married at the end of his assignment.

Having always enjoyed an almost supernatural twin connection, making sense of his brother's feelings had been a little disconcerting. He'd picked up on a lot of awe, wonder, confusion and frustration. It wasn't until Jeb's, er, *physical release*—orgasms had never been a secret, a fact that had been quite embarrassing in their teens—that Judd had realized that his brother had fallen head over heels in love. Though he didn't experience the sensations as strongly as Jeb— more shadowed and less profound than the original— he'd found himself a little envious of his twin.

Not envious enough to want to permanently shackle himself to a member of the opposite sex though. He'd come damned close to that in his last year at West Point, a mistake he didn't ever intend to make again. He smothered a dark chuckle.

Fool me once…was enough. Lesson learned.

Naturally he knew that all women weren't faithless money-grubbing connivers, like the one who'd almost tricked him into an until-death-do-you-part, but knowing it and having it make a difference were two different things.

Heather had studied him, understood his weaknesses and knew exactly what to say and do to appeal to his "hero" complex. In the end, his "damaged fragile flower in need of a protector" had been a two-time divorcée with multiple aliases and a rap sheet longer than the damned Declaration of Independence. And he'd nearly brought that viper into their family? His lips quirked.

They already had one of those, thank you very much—his grandmother.

The matriarch of the family and the formidable

head of Anderson Enterprises, Twila Anderson was notoriously hard and could hold a grudge and her own opinion longer than anyone he'd ever known. She no longer had the ability to scare the hell out of him, but if he'd wanted to continue taking orders he would have stayed in the military. Though he could have gone to work for her, or any one of the company's holdings, Judd had ultimately, once again, decided to follow in his brother's footsteps.

Contrary to popular belief, he *did* have an original thought and they *didn't* share a mind, but they were so closely tied to one another that living independently of the other was simply…unpleasant. They were more than brothers, they were best friends. And while Jeb had left the military after that horrible disaster in Mosul, Judd had actually been considering it before his brother had.

A sniper who couldn't pull the trigger was essentially useless and, given that it had gotten increasingly more difficult with every target…

And the hell of it? He had no earthly idea why.

Judd had always prided himself on being able to do the hard job—making the conscious decision to end another person's life was not easy, even if it was justified. Men who intentionally killed, mutilated and maimed innocent women and children were lower than pond scum and didn't deserve to live, dammit.

For every one of those people he finished off, he'd always congratulated himself with the lives he'd saved.

The end justified the means, the greater good and all of that. And he still believed it—he really did—but doing it… Putting a man in the crosshairs, making the kill shot. That was out of reach. He couldn't do it anymore.

Not that he'd confided that to anyone—even Jeb. It was too galling, too shameful. Better that they thought he missed his twin than the truth.

Initially, he'd chalked his hesitation up to burnout—it happened. He'd taken a short leave to Crete—he hadn't had time to come home and wouldn't have even if he could—but even the island paradise, lots of good sex, good food and good wine hadn't made a difference.

He was done. His career in the military was over.

Luckily, Jeb had paved the way with Ranger Security and Judd couldn't have been any more thankful. Owners and legendary Rangers Jamie Flanagan, Brian Payne and Guy McCann were the collective best of what Uncle Sam had to offer. Coolly efficient with an unmatched attention to detail, Payne had been nicknamed The Specialist and the moniker more than fit. With a rumored genius IQ and enough brawn to strike fear into the bravest of men, Flanagan had met and married Colonel Carl Garrett's granddaughter, which was proof enough of his courage. And McCann's mystical ability to surf the fine line between brilliance and stupidity and always land in hero territory had made him locker room lore.

Added to the fact that these men were former soldiers—and more significantly, Rangers—it made this job the perfect fit. Because he'd never been stateside long enough to outfit a permanent residence, Judd was thankful for the furnished apartment that came with his generous employment package and looked forward to finding a place of his own.

His new sister-in-law, Sophie, had even offered to deed him off some acreage from her farm, where she and Jeb had made their home. Admittedly, it was tempting, if for no other reason than it would make his brother his neighbor. And since he suspected that a little Sophie or Jeb wouldn't be too long in the making, being the "fun uncle" held immense appeal.

A tinkle of low, feminine laughter sounded through the door, ringing an internal hum of awareness along his nerve endings. An unfamiliar prickling tightened the skin on the tops of his fingers, made his stomach clench. He frowned, shaking the bizarre sensation off, and focused on the job at hand. A quick glance along both ends of the street confirmed that he wasn't being watched and that all was well. Judd pretended to check the address on the package he carried against the house number, then knocked on the door.

Utter silence. The laughing stopped as though a switch had been thrown.

He heard the soft shuffle of a heavy foot across carpet, could feel someone staring at him through the peephole and held up the box. "Bluebird Services. I'm here to deliver a package."

"Perishable or non-perishable?" a voice asked, verifying the security question.

"Perishable," he confirmed.

Judd listened as a series of locks disengaged, then the door opened to reveal a rangy officer with more hair on his face than his head. His eyes were guarded, a little regretful and mildly relieved. No doubt keeping this key witness out of harm's way was the most exciting bit of police work Officer ZZ Top had ever done, Judd thought, following him inside the house.

In keeping with the generally shabby appearance of the outside, the interior was equally depressed. Stained brown carpet covered the floors, dated brown paneling lined the walls and bare bulbs hung from the dingy water-stained—okay, fine, *brown*—ceiling. Wearing uniforms the color of ditch water, the three officers matched the bleak decor.

Which was probably what made the woman standing in the middle of them all the more remarkable.

She stood out like a flamingo in a flock of cow-birds.

His heart began to pound, pushing the blood through his veins so fast that his mouth parched. A peculiar feeling fluttered through his chest, not altogether unpleasant, and the centers of his palms tingled with heat. He couldn't have been any more surprised if fireballs emerged from them. Though he knew it hadn't, the floor felt like it shifted beneath his feet and his stomach suddenly floated inside his belly with breathless anticipation, the same way it did the instant he jumped out of a plane. He swallowed, shaken.

It was…disconcerting.

Tall and willowy with long, blazing red hair that gleamed with vitality despite the lack of proper lighting, she practically glowed from within, bathing the rest of the world around her with her illumination. Her skin was pale and peachy-looking, her mouth a small but ripe raspberry pink that immediately put him in mind of sex, and delicate brows arched over a pair of particularly startling green eyes. They were light, the color of antique glass, and heavily fringed with dark auburn lashes. She wore a long multi-colored skirt which clung to an especially nice ass, a white tunic with billowy sleeves, lots of noisy jewelry—it jingled with every move she made—and a pair of fuzzy pink bunny slippers on her feet. The scent of meat loaf and apple pie hung in the air and a small candle burned on the battered coffee table.

What was more startling was what she was doing—cutting one of the officers' hair, of all things. While she worked, she did a lot of humming under her breath, biting her distracting lips and frowning critically. She didn't look the least bit concerned that someone was trying to kill her. In fact, she just looked…busy. A quick glance revealed that everyone but ZZ Top had gotten a fresh trim and shave.

"I'm almost done," she said, without looking up. *Snip, snip, snip.* Frown. *Snip, snip, snip.* "See, Roy, the trick is to condition regularly. Hair is hair. Just because you're a man doesn't mean your hair doesn't need a decent moisturizer, especially with all this curl," she said, pushing her hands through it with a little groan of delight that made his balls tighten.

Roy's, too, by the look of him.

A fair baby-faced blonde with more than a spare tire hanging over his belt, dear old Roy blushed to the roots of the hair she presently worked on.

"I bet the girls just can't get enough of those curls, can they?" she continued, smiling as she tweaked a few more strands. "It's a good thing you don't have any dimples, Roy, because dimples *and* curls would have made you downright irresistible, and that's hardly fair to any of the rest of the men in this town, is it?"

"Right," one of the men drawled. "'Cause he beats them off with a stick now, doesn't he?"

She looked up and sent the offender a scowl that managed to be as quelling as it was disappointed. "*Clark.*"

Clark's smug smile instantly fell and he reached down and popped a rubber band against his wrist. "Sarcasm isn't a weapon," he said, seemingly by rote. "I can be clever without being cruel."

Judd blinked, stunned. *What the hell...?*

She beamed approvingly at Clark, her pale green eyes lighting with pleasure. "Intelligence is attractive, but only when it's put to good use. Wouldn't it be a shame to waste that fine mind, Clark? Have you given any more thought to going back to school, pursuing that dream of architecture we talked about?"

Clark glanced at the floor and sheepishly shuffled his feet. "I'm still thinking about it."

"Thinking is good, but taking action is better. Make the choice and commit to it." She smiled indulgently. "You know you can do it."

What was she? Judd wondered. Some sort of life coach? A daytime TV junkie? Both?

"You're determined to make sure that I'm an of-

ficer short on my police force, aren't you?" ZZ Top
scolded with a good-natured grimace.

She rolled her eyes as she continued to work on
Roy's curly hair. "As if you couldn't handle the whole
thing by yourself," she said fondly. "You're so efficient, you've shaved all the hair right off your head to
keep from having to fix it. I hope Mossy Ridge appre-
ciates you, Les. You do a fine job. Just like that lovely
wife of yours, this community is lucky to have you."

Les's chest puffed with pride and he ran a hand
over his bald head, which had turned decidedly pink.

Any minute now Judd fully expected all three men
to jump up, start dancing in circles around her and
break into "Whistle While You Work." But she wasn't
Snow White, they weren't dwarves and he sure as
hell wasn't Prince Charming, though he had been accused of being the Prince of Darkness a time or two.

"Ms. Montgomery, I'm Judd Anderson, your security specialist. I'm here to escort you to your permanent location while you await the trial. Please collect
your things. We need to go."

There, Judd thought. Firm but polite, the equiva-
lent of *Move your ass, please.*

She stilled and finally, very slowly, looked up at
him. Though he was too well-trained to betray an
inkling of unease, the force of that droll green gaze
when it met his was nothing short of…cataclysmic.

Like a tsunami meeting a hurricane, an earthquake in the middle of a tornado, planets colliding in space. He felt like he'd been sucked into the resulting vacuum, powerless as a whole new galaxy formed around him...and he was staring directly at its princess.

Predictably, his cell phone vibrated from his front pocket—Jeb, no doubt, because there was no way in hell he wasn't picking up on that little emotional anomaly. He didn't know when he'd ever been so affected, when he'd ever simply looked into a pair of eyes—admittedly, very pretty ones—and felt the earth move. An inexplicable coil of heat spiraled into his loins, curling around his dick, and his fingers twitched with the urge to touch her, to run the pad of his thumb over her bottom lip.

"I understand that you've recently left the military," she said, her tone conciliatory, as though she were speaking to a sullen teenager, "and adjusting your demeanor to your new civilian life might be a bit of a struggle. But your transition would be a lot smoother if you were to remember that you're no longer at liberty to issue orders and no one you speak to is obliged to follow them." The barest hint of irritation flashed in her gaze. "Most particularly *me*," she added.

Clark, Les and Roy all chuckled, then quickly turned their amusement into fake coughs when she shot them another one of those mysterious glances that somehow, to his utter astonishment, turned the three into awkward ball-less wonders.

Evidently she figured she was going to be able to do the same thing with him, Judd thought, feeling his jaw involuntarily clench. Perfect. Now *all* of him was hard. But if she thought she was going to be able to dress him down and wrap him around her little finger as easily as she had these hapless fools, then she'd better think again.

Oh, hell, no.

Better to disabuse her of that notion *toute suite*.

He smiled at her, twisted his lips just enough to be patronizing. "Since we both speak English and understand the language, communication, obviously, isn't an issue. This is more of a comprehension problem. I apologize," he said with a small nod. "Where I stated the facts, you heard an order. In future, I'll make sure you understand the difference."

He straightened, going into Obedience or Death mode, and looked at each of the men in turn. "Les, check the perimeter. Roy, call your lookouts for an update. Clark, sweep the street. There were twelve vehicles and a motorcycle when I arrived. One mini-van, six sedans, two trucks, three SUVs and a Harley Davidson. If there's a change in any status quo, I want to know it. Move."

They all scattered and bolted into action. Satisfied, Judd turned to look at her. "Those were orders," he explained patiently, in the same condescending tone she'd used. "They followed them because it's their job, just like it's my job to keep you safe. Any directive I issue is for your protection, Ms. Montgomery, not for my amusement or due to my lack of understanding the difference between military and civilian cultures. I'm not obliged to say *please* or ask nicely and, so we're clear, I don't work for you. I work for Ranger Security. Ranger Security works for the client, Ed Johnson, who hired the company to protect you at all costs." He lifted a brow. "With me so far?"

Her lips curled into a smile that more resembled a snarl and her entire body seemed to vibrate with anger. For whatever reason, Judd got the impression that he'd just awakened a dormant volcano. Perversely, he looked forward to the eruption. "Oh, I think I can grasp the concept. You're in charge."

He nodded and grinned at her, enjoying this much more than he should have. "See?" he said, rocking back on his heels. "Not too difficult. Now get your things," he repeated. "We need to leave."

Her eyes narrowed fractionally. "Right."

Imagining he could see the steam billowing from the top of her head, she turned abruptly on her heel and left the room.

He released a pent-up breath, one he didn't even realize he'd been holding. Four days, he thought as a blaze of heat kindled in his loins, the memory of her mouth making his own water.

Four days. Alone. With her.

God help him.

2

OF ALL THE unmitigated nerve, Noelle thought, seething as she angrily slung her things into a bag. Had she ever met a more provoking man? One that, with a mere slightly condescending smile and a handful of words, had turned her mind purple with rage?

On purpose.

Honestly, she'd always prided herself on her ability to get along with almost anybody, on never allowing herself to be goaded into an argument or unpleasantness because, nine times out of ten, the instigator didn't argue to make a point, but to sling mud. Noelle had never minded getting dirty—she'd done a tour with the Peace Corps, had dug wells in Africa, helped build schools in Guatemala, had worked clean up after hurricanes, earthquakes and tornadoes. She'd worked in countless soup kitchens, free clinics and homeless shelters. Service was her passion, her gift, and it fulfilled her in ways that the people closest to her had never understood.

Like her parents, who'd basically turned over her admittedly sizable trust fund, then washed their hands of her. "Fine, Noelle," her father had said, exasperated and angry. "You win. I'll go ahead and sign over the money. And when you've given it away to every bleeding heart group in the world and saved every endangered animal on the planet—when it's all gone and you have no other choice—maybe then you'll grow up and get a *real* job like the rest of us."

That dart had penetrated because she did work— *hard,* dammit—but she was paid in kindness rather than cash, satisfaction in lieu of a check. And why shouldn't she be able to do what she wanted? Thanks to her grandparents who'd put the money away for her after hitting a seven-million dollar jackpot in a Vegas slot machine, she could afford to serve others, to offer a little financial assistance to causes she cared about. She'd paid cash for her modest house, had no debt and had socked away a good portion in an investment portfolio which, even in this poor economy, still made her plenty of money.

Hell, she wasn't stupid. She was just different.

It pained her that her mother and father had never understood her, that they weren't proud of her, that ultimately, the way she'd chosen to live her life had disappointed them and caused a rift. Other than the obligatory cards at Christmas and on her birthday—which happened to be on the same day, thus her name—she hadn't heard from them in more than two years and each time the postmark was from a different part of the world.

Christmas, probably due to it being her birthday, was always particularly tough. Because when the volunteering was over and every hungry mouth had been fed, in the end she was still in front of a lonely tree, opening the two presents she'd ultimately bought for herself and singing a mash-up version of "Jingle Bells" and "Happy Birthday." Her parents hadn't even bothered to send a gift last year, but had just stuck a check into the card that had arrived a week early. From Morocco. Though her father loved to tout the get-a-real-job idea to her, he'd fully embraced early retirement. Her lips tilted. She often wondered if the air was thinner up where he sat on top of his high horse.

Though she knew it was petty, she hadn't made an effort to get in touch with them and let them know that she was the single witness to a high-profile crime, that the infamous Winchester clan of Calgary county had tried to kill her three times in the past four months—the bulk of which had happened in the last few weeks—to keep her from giving testimony in court.

Noelle had never given too much thought to her own death until someone had deliberately attempted to take her life. The resulting terror and anger had been nothing short of enlightening. Not only had it put her in touch with her own mortality, it had forced her to reevaluate her very existence, to measure her days in minutes rather than hours. She'd always lived by the "do the next right thing" mantra, but it seemed even more significant now. Even more important to make sure that her life, however humble or short, made a difference.

And though she'd consoled grieving parents after the last three world disasters and had held the hand of a dying child who'd been belatedly pulled from the rubble of a recent tornado in Alabama, she'd never witnessed a deliberate death.

An execution.

Both were senseless, but the latter haunted her to no end. Perhaps because the tornado had been a freak of nature and the murder...had not. The end of Rupert Nichols's life had been cold-blooded and merciless. It had been ended over something as trivial as a differing opinion on a brand of ketchup, she'd later find out.

Travis "Tubby" Winchester—the nickname was a throwback to his elementary school days when he'd evidently had a bit of a weight problem—had pulled Rupert Nichols out the back door of his Main Street café, forced him to his knees, casually put a gun between Rupert's eyes, said, "Nobody argues with me. *I'm* the Decider," and then pulled the trigger. He'd adjusted his jacket, pocketed the weapon, then climbed back into his waiting car and driven away as though nothing had happened.

Noelle had seen all of this from her vantage point behind a parked car. She'd been volunteering at the free clinic on the other side of the alley and had noticed a pair of unusually small, malnourished kittens when she'd come in earlier in the day. She'd put out some food for them and had planned to look for them when she'd finished her shift. That's what she'd been doing in the alley when Tubby's car had pulled in. She'd been wedged up under the back tire of an SUV, trying to coax the kittens from beneath the vehicle with a piece of beef jerky when she'd heard Rupert's initial cry.

It's odd the thoughts that flip through a person's mind when faced with a horrible situation. For instance, when Tubby's car had driven past, she'd been more worried about the cats darting under one of his tires than being seen by the legendary local crime boss, that beef jerky had been a poor choice to lure the kittens in the first place and how having a little packet of tuna in her purse wouldn't be remiss for times like this.

It was as though her brain had been trying to think of anything but the dead man across the way.

She'd scrambled from her inadvertent hiding place, falling once in the process and tearing a hole in her jeans, then stumbled toward him, her heart pounding in her suddenly roaring ears. She'd known he was gone—that the neat hole between his sightless eyes was deceptively small for all the damage it had done—but the impulse to help, to do something was too strong to ignore. A lump welled in her throat.

In the end, all she could do was close his eyes and dial 911.

Having made her home in Mossy Ridge during her childhood and teens, then as her "base camp" when she was between volunteer and relief postings, Noelle knew Rupert well. He'd been her Little League soccer coach, was allergic to fire ants and lived in a gray-and-white Cape Cod style house a couple of streets over from her own place. The Main Street Diner had been in his family for as long as she could remember and, while it was never going to be famous, the café served a good meat loaf and had the best banana pudding this side of the Mason-Dixon line.

His family, understandably, had been devastated.

Thankfully, during those awful seconds just after

the shooting, Noelle had had the presence of mind to get a look at the license plate. She'd always had a good mind for numbers—could still remember her locker combination from high school—and while her eye witness account might have been questionable considering her position, poor lighting and a host of other factors, knowing that number had solidified her as a credible witness.

The district attorney, who'd been trying to nail Tubby on a cache of other crimes he'd managed to wiggle out of, had been practically giddy with excitement. While he'd managed to put away some of the notorious crime boss's underlings for various offenses—drugs, prostitution, racketeering, even murder—he'd never been able to get a single one of them to turn state's evidence against their leader.

And now, thanks to her, their leader was in custody.

In a bold move that had ultimately sent his family into hiding, the presiding judge had revoked bond and no amount of threatening or a well-argued point from one of Tubby's exorbitantly expensive attorneys had been able to convince him otherwise. Tubby had been remanded until trial and that, as they say, was that.

But it hadn't kept him from putting a hit out on her and Noelle had known that every day closer to the trial date put her closer and closer to danger. Tubby and his crime family hadn't been able to avoid the law for this long because they were innocent—it was because most people didn't have the nerve to confront them or put their own families at risk. But Noelle didn't have any family close enough for them to use as leverage—she tried not to consider how sad that was—and she'd thought too much of Rupert to be bullied or frightened into silence.

When the threatening letters and phone calls had started, she hadn't been surprised. Though shaken, she'd installed a top of the line security system, added a canister of mace to her key chain and a gun to her purse, then had brushed up on her self-defense skills.

But when someone had taken a shot at her outside the local Piggly Wiggly—she and her Pink Lady apples had fallen to the ground when the window behind her had shattered, resulting in bruises on *both* of them—that's when she'd really gotten unnerved. A second shot had blasted through her living room window the following week, and the only thing that had prevented her death was the fact that she'd bent forward to retrieve the remote control from the coffee table so that she could rewind *Pride and Prejudice* and watch Mr. Darcy strip down and dive into the lake again.

She'd forever credit Colin Firth and Jane Austen for saving her life.

But this last attempt had terrified her even more. Evidently having decided that there was too much room for error with a bullet, her attackers had hurled a Molotov cocktail through her kitchen window and tried to burn her to death. She'd shoved Lilo and Stitch, her new kittens, into a pillow case, much to their howling displeasure, and climbed out the upper-story window of her guest bedroom. Thankfully, she'd neglected to cut away a tree limb that had grown too close and she was able to scramble to safety.

It was at that point that Ed Johnson, one of her oldest and dearest friends from their local Red Cross agency, had stepped in and hired Ranger Security. Mossy Ridge's tiny police force didn't have the manpower or the preparedness to deal with this sort of issue. According to Ed, a former military man himself, Ranger Security was the best in the business and he was confident in their ability to keep her out of harm's way. Noelle released a small, shaky breath as a burst of heat mushroomed slowly inside her once more.

Clearly she and Ed had differing definitions on what exactly constituted "safe."

Because she'd felt many things when she'd looked up and caught a glimpse of Judd Anderson, but interestingly enough, *safe* wasn't one of them. Truth be told, she hadn't even had to look up. The instant he'd walked into the room, she'd felt the change in the atmosphere, a significant recalculation to her own personal barometer. A strangely pleasant sort of pressure had invaded the shabby but cozy space, making it difficult to breathe and the fine hairs on her body had prickled to attention, a testament to his particular energy.

It was unnerving.

Noelle had known before she fully looked up that he was going to be handsome. The bits of him she'd seen from the corner of her eye had been proof enough of that. He'd practically filled the doorway, leaving little space between the top and sides of the frame. She'd caught a glimpse of dark hair, massive shoulders, lean hips and long legs and, though the courier's uniform was supposed to lend credibility to his ruse, something about the outfit on him put her in mind of a male stripper. She'd mentally queued "Sexy and I Know It" and waited for him to rip his pants off.

Then he'd spoken in that unbelievably autocratic my-way-or-the-highway tone and ruined it all.

In quite possibly the sexiest voice she'd ever heard, which was hardly fair. It put her in mind of velvet and satin, the rustle of sheets, naked skin and hot bodies. Sex, frankly. Which she hadn't had in more than a year, after the disintegration of her last slightly serious relationship.

And then she'd looked up into those impossibly dark eyes—so dark, in fact, that she couldn't automatically distinguish pupil from iris, and the effect had been nothing short of breathtaking. Her brain had momentarily short-circuited and blanked of all pertinent content. A blaze of awareness fired over her skin, leaving her flushed and flustered and, though she knew she hadn't moved, she felt a bit like Alice, tumbling counter clockwise down the rabbit hole.

Never a stranger to embarrassment, Noelle had often wished for the ground to open up beneath her feet and swallow her whole, but this was a decidedly different occasion and the sensation was more than a little disconcerting because she had the irrational idea that *he* should be tumbling with her and instead of a hole, they should fall into bed and not get out of it until he'd had her for breakfast, lunch and dinner.

Or some approximation thereof.

Which was another anomaly because she'd never simply looked at a man and…melted. Or vibrated. Or tingled. In her lady bits. Without some other form of stimulation.

Her nipples puckered even now, remembering.

Because she was used to being the master of herself and, as often as possible, everyone else around her—life was simply easier that way—she'd managed to get a hold of herself and issue the set down Mr. High and Mighty Soldier deserved. He wasn't her superior officer and she hadn't appreciated his tone. In her experience, kindness was almost always more effective than being domineering. She liked to build people up, to challenge them to be better.

Like Les and Roy and Clark, for instance. Les didn't recognize his own honor or efficiency, Roy simply needed to look in the mirror and find something to love about himself and Clark's keen mind had been conditioned to insult others instead of bettering himself. In the two weeks they'd been protecting her, she thought she'd made a good deal of progress. It was easy enough to do if one bothered to look for the good and illustrate it to others.

That was her strength, *that's* what made her a good volunteer, a good ambassador for kindness. She could strip the hide off of someone with the sharpness of her tongue, if necessary, but she'd rather not. Arguing or giving in to irritation was easy—lazy, even, if you asked her—but *not* arguing or controlling one's temper took effort.

The fact that she'd not only lost her temper in her very first exchange with her new security guard—and then lost the verbal war—wasn't an encouraging sign of things to come. Coupled with her irrational, wholly thrilling but definitely unwise reaction to him—the tingling had migrated to more sensitive areas below her waist—and Noelle knew she was really in trouble.

Quite possibly, much to her surprise, even out of her depth. Had she ever been out of her depth, she wondered absently, a frown inching across her brow. Had she ever met anyone who'd put her so firmly off her game? She blinked, mildly alarmed.

No.

The singular difference between most intelligent people was the decisions they ultimately chose to make. Her mouth puckered with grim determination. And she wasn't going to make one now that would put her into the Brilliant but Unforgivably Stupid category.

She couldn't afford to be stupid, unforgivably or otherwise, and she was quite sure that the situation she presently found herself in wasn't going to magically rectify itself without any action on her part. So…

It had to be done.

With a resigned sigh and a violent twinge of irrational disappointment, Noelle picked up her cell phone, powered it on, and then dialed directory assistance. "Atlanta, Georgia," she said. "Ranger Security." She straightened when someone who identified himself as Juan-Carlos answered the phone. "Good afternoon, Juan-Carlos. My name is Noelle Montgomery and I'd like to request a different agent. Who would I need to talk to about that?"

3

Les, Roy and Clark had all reported in, with satisfactory results, and given the all clear for him and Noelle—the name definitely suited her, he thought—to quickly make their move. He glanced at his watch and inwardly groaned.

Which they could do if she'd simply *move*.

Honestly, how long did it take to put a few things in a bag? It wasn't as if she hadn't known when he was coming. She should have already been packed and ready, if you asked Judd, but no. No, no, no. Snow White had been too busy making homemade apple pie and giving her staunch protectors a makeover to worry about making it easier for him to keep her safe.

It boggled the mind.

Had he ever met anyone so… So… He wracked his brain for the right word and couldn't find one.

She defied description.

Other than being extraordinarily, almost supernaturally hot, of course. And given the heat still bubbling in the bottom of his loins, it was a miracle this hideously ugly pair of polyester pants hadn't melted through the crotch. Had he caught the scent of scorching fabric, he wouldn't have been in the least surprised.

Exasperated and eager to get on the road, Judd heaved a sigh and made his way to her door. He rapped a couple of times. "Ms. Montgomery, would you like some help?"

"Er...no," she said, sounding oddly distracted. She mumbled something low, almost as though she was talking to someone else.

He frowned, a finger of unease nudging his belly. "Not to belabor the point, but as I've said, it's important that we get on the road. The quicker we act, the better." He was not going to ask her to hurry. That went without saying and, as she seemed to be fiendishly clever, she knew that already.

It was infuriating.

Her voice, when it came, was from farther away than before. "I'm almost finished," she said. Had she moved? All the way across the room? And if so, then why? He heard her mutter a low, heartfelt curse.

"I'll help you," he said, grabbing the doorknob. He

realized it was locked at the exact same moment that his cell phone vibrated. He swore under his breath, checked the display, fully anticipating another message from his twin, then blinked when he realized it was the office calling—Payne's direct line, as a matter of fact.

"Anderson," he answered with a puzzled frown. Surely to God he hadn't screwed something up already. Hell, he'd just gotten here.

"Afternoon, Judd," Payne said, a hint of something not readily definable in his cool voice. Irony, maybe? Humor certainly. "How's it going?"

"It's all clear," he said. "I'm merely waiting on Ms. Montgomery to collect her belongings so that we can be on our way. She'd neglected to pack," he said a little loudly, in a slightly dark tone, hoping to shame her into action.

Strangely enough, his boss cleared his throat of a chuckle. "Right. Where is she, exactly?"

Judd scowled again, glanced at the door as though he could suddenly see through it. What an odd question. "She's in her room."

"Ah, that explains it," Payne said.

Explained what? Because he was as confused as hell. "I'm sorry?"

"Your target just called and asked for a new agent.

Evidently she's decided that you and she aren't going to get along. You're 'ill-suited,' she said."

Shock detonated through him, widening his eyes. "She *what?*"

"I know that this is your first assignment for us, Judd, and I know I don't need to tell you how to do your job—truthfully, this is the first time this has ever happened—but in future I think it would probably be best not to let her out of your sight. And you should confiscate her cell phone. She doesn't need one while she's in your custody and they're too easily traced. Tubby Winchester is no fool, despite his name, and he's connected with exceedingly deep pockets. Tracking her via the GPS in her mobile is completely within the scope of his range."

Judd's jaw clenched so hard he feared it would shatter and he glared a black, blistering hole at the door. Mortification momentarily robbed him of speech. His face and temper equally flamed. "Right," he bit out.

"As I explained to Ms. Montgomery, you were the agent chosen for this case because you were best suited to this job and merely swapping you out, even if it was possible—which it isn't—wouldn't be in her best interests. I advised her to follow your instruction to the letter."

She'd *tattled* on him, Judd thought, still stunned

and impossibly angrier than he had been only seconds before. His nostrils flared. His blood pressure inched toward stroke level. Like he was some sort of damned bully on the playground. "Thank you, sir."

"Whoa," his boss said. "I'm no 'sir.' I'm either Brian or Payne. Your choice because I'll answer to both. And, so we're clear, you aren't being called on the carpet, you're being apprised of the situation." He laughed softly under his breath. "Good luck," he said. "She sounds like she's going to be a little hard to handle." He paused thoughtfully. "I don't think I've ever been so flattered while having my judgment questioned."

Ah, yes. He was familiar with the technique. "Neat trick, that, isn't it?" Judd asked with a grim laugh. He was still steaming over the military vs. civilian culture insinuation. Well, if she'd found his communication skills lacking before, then she'd better brace herself…because things were about to get a whole lot worse.

After assuring Payne that he would text when they reached the safe house—which was actually a rented cabin in the north Georgia mountains—he disconnected and, with a well-placed kick of his boot, easily popped the door past the meager lock. It swung open on its hinges, revealing a wide-eyed and gratifyingly startled Noelle Montgomery.

She blinked. Swallowed.

Then, naturally—determinedly—lifted her chin. For reasons which escaped him, he found that unimaginably sexy. Hot. Infuriating. "You could have simply asked me to unlock the door," she said. With an unconcerned shrug, she picked up her purse from off the bed and swung it over her slim shoulder. "But you definitely get an A-plus for dramatic effect."

That *tone*. That dismissive, unimpressed, pat-on-the-head-now-go-play-with-your-toys-little-boy *tone* literally made his eye twitch.

Judd strode forward, ignoring the rapid increase in his pulse and the sulky pout of her bottom lip, then plucked her cell phone from the front panel of her bag, turned it off and slipped it into his pocket.

She inhaled sharply. "That was mine," she said through clenched teeth.

"I'm aware," he growled.

"Listen, Jack, I don't know who you think you are, but—"

Before she could finish the rest of that sentence, Judd picked her up and slung her over his shoulder in a fireman hold—disregarding her muffled sound of outraged protest—then grabbed her bag and headed for the door. She smelled like a Christmas cookie, like butter and vanilla frosting. Insanely, his mouth watered for a taste of her. A lick, a nibble, even a painless little bite.

"Wait! Stop!" she yelled, frantically grabbing hold of the frame as they went through. "Lilo and Stitch!"

He paused and cocked his head toward her rump. Mistake. It was a nice rump. Mouthwatering. He gave his head a shake. "What? You've got a Disney movie in here somewhere?"

"No, you gigantic jackass," she hissed, exasperated. "The basket in the corner. My kittens."

His brow creased with confusion. "What?"

She wiggled, evidently trying to propel him into the other direction. "My kittens!" she repeated impatiently. "I'm not leaving without them."

"No, she's not," Les announced from directly in front of him. His expression wavered between amused and concerned, a smile finally winning out. "I'm allergic."

Right, Judd thought. And he was Santa Claus.

"Kittens," Judd repeated tonelessly. "Wonderful."

Ignoring temptation, he took a couple of steps back to avoid whacking her head against the door frame, then made his way to the corner where the innocuous-looking wicker basket sat. He squatted down, carefully lifted the lid and dual sets of bright green eyes peered back at him from little black, whiskered faces. He sighed and resisted the urge to pass a hand over his face. He'd gone from picking off terrorists one at a time to babysitting kittens and an ungrateful eyewitness who'd lobbied within minutes of meeting him to get him replaced.

Perfect. Perhaps leaving the military had been a mistake, Judd thought with a fatalistic grunt.

"I'm not going without them," she repeated stubbornly, an undercurrent of panic in her voice.

Les wandered over, closed the lid, lifted the basket and then turned and handed it to Noelle. "Of course not, darlin'. They're yours, aren't they?"

She crooned something nonsensical and ground the edge of the container into his back. On purpose, he suspected.

"Fine," he said. He straightened and made the return trek through the house, listening as she promised to get in touch with all of them as soon as the trial was over to see how they were doing. She thanked them for taking such good care of her, adding, "I don't think I can expect as good a treatment from my new guard," her voice ebbing and flowing with each determined step that he took.

As if he were her damned jailer and not there for her protection. Honest to God, by the time he got her out of here, there wasn't going to be a bit of enamel left on his back teeth.

"Is this really necessary?" Clark asked, arching

a questioning brow as they came through the living room.

"He's showing off, Clark. Where you use words, my hero here prefers brute force," she drawled. "No doubt he's overcompensating," she stage-whispered loudly.

She was in the wrong position for throttling, but a spanking wasn't out of the question, he thought, seething. "The only thing I'm overcompensating for is her pure lack of preparedness," Judd remarked. "Evidently, Ms. Montgomery has as little regard for our lives as she does her own, otherwise she would have been ready and cooperative when I got here. And she wouldn't have used her cell phone—which she shouldn't have been allowed to keep anyway— and possibly compromised all of you by giving her hunters an opportunity to locate her via the GPS mechanism in her phone. I'd clear out quickly if I were you," he advised them.

Silence, at last. A chink in the armor?

Roy accommodatingly opened the door for him. "Keep safe, Noelle," he said, concern coloring his tone. "Merry Christmas."

"Merry Christmas, boys," she repeated wistfully. "I'll be in touch when I can."

Her soft breasts bounced against his back as he descended the steps and started down the walk.

"Oh, yes," she said mockingly. "I can see where you hauling me across the yard like a caveman isn't the least bit conspicuous. Gee, I wonder why no one else thought of this? You would have attracted less attention if you'd dragged me by my hair."

He opened the door, tossed her bag into the back and dumped her unceremoniously into the passenger seat. She huffed a breath, adjusted her skirt, then strapped both herself and the basket in behind the seat belt.

Judd braced both hands on the doorframe and leaned forward, delighted when she gulped, and bared his teeth in a grin. "Oh, don't worry, Princess Pain in the Ass. That's how I plan to get you inside."

"SHE ASKED FOR a different agent?" Jeb Anderson parroted, shock racing across the features that couldn't be any more different than his twin's. "Seriously?"

Payne chuckled softly and shook his head. "Yes, she did. Your brother sounded immensely displeased."

Jeb grunted knowingly. "I'll bet he did." He whistled low. "I'm the more even-keeled of the two of us," he said. "My mother used to tease us, saying I was the dynamite and Judd was the explosion."

He could certainly see that, Payne thought. Jeb had reminded him strongly of himself—controlled, measured and meticulous. Banked energy. Judd, on the other hand, was like a live wire. Thought and action were so seamlessly tied together that one might assume that he didn't make the proper considerations before proceeding. But that assumption would be wrong. Judd Anderson always knew what he was doing and why he was doing it.

And seeing the pair of them together was definitely bizarre. Heaven and Hell, Guy had joked. Where Jeb resembled an angel fallen from Paradise—blond hair and blue-eyed—Judd looked like he'd been spit straight out the gates of Hades. Jet black hair, even blacker eyes. Add in their size—which was notable—and the fact that Jeb was right handed, with a remarkable dimple in his right cheek and Judd was left-handed and that same dimple cut through his left cheek…it was striking. Were that not enough to make them two of the most interesting people he'd ever met, the pair had the strongest twin connection Payne had ever seen. They didn't just finish each other's sentences or communicate with some sort of silent language, they could pick up on what the other was feeling. They had a hypersensitive bond that boggled the mind.

Furthermore, though Jeb had seemed content and relatively settled—particularly after meeting and marrying Sophie—since coming on board at the agency, the difference in him now that Judd was here as well was especially notable. He laughed more easily, smiled more readily and seemed generally more at ease. "Friends from the womb," Jeb had explained, when Payne had mentioned the change to him.

Jeb glanced up at him, hesitated. "He's keeping something from me," he said. "I know it."

He would, Payne thought. He had a feeling he knew where this conversation was going. "Oh?"

"I know that when I left things were a bit…difficult for him. For me as well," he added. "Not that we couldn't handle it, of course. But…" He glanced at the carpet, shrugged. "Not to get too woo-woo on you," he said, describing the twin connection. "But managing the twin thing is just easier when we're closer. Being on different continents for the past nine months has been a little stressful for both of us."

Payne nodded. "I can see where that would be true."

"Our parents think Judd left the military because he couldn't bear to be away from me. That's true, in part, I'm sure." He glanced up, leveled his gaze at him. "But there's something more. Another reason. Something else happened. I *know* it. *Feel* it. But whatever it is, he hasn't shared it with me. We've never kept secrets from each other." His lips twisted with wry humor. "Why bother, right?" he joked. "But he's keeping one now and I know that whatever it is…it's unpleasant for him." He paused, speared Payne with another one of those direct looks. "I know you've talked to Colonel Garrett. Could you shed any light on the situation for me?"

And there it was. He'd anticipated this discussion and as such had prepared his answer. "I'd rather not," Payne told him. "What I'm aware of didn't come from your brother, so strictly speaking it wouldn't be a betrayal of trust. But speaking as a man and former soldier with my own private struggles, there are some things that are better shared in one's own time, wouldn't you agree?"

Payne knew he would, because Jeb's reasons for leaving the military had been so similar to his own. Botched mission, lost lives, the burden of responsibility and shame. Payne had eventually come to terms with his own guilt and suspected that Jeb was on his way there as well, but the path was long and arduous. The same qualities that made a man a good soldier were the very same ones that made him honorable and self-sacrificing. The mantle of responsibility was heavy and grew even weightier when something went wrong. He thumped his pen absently against his desk, inwardly grimacing. Shrugging that bitch off when it landed on your shoulders was damned tough.

Jeb was thoughtful for a moment, then eventually smiled and lifted his shoulder. "I had to try," he said.

Payne chuckled. "I would have done the same."

"Ah, hell," Jeb muttered with a sigh. "I guess he's entitled to one secret."

"He'll eventually tell you. Keeping it from you is probably harder than actually sharing it."

Jeb paused to consider him, his gaze direct and thoughtful. "I think you have a better understanding of this than most experts claim to," he remarked.

Payne merely shrugged. "People are fascinating."

And Jeb and Judd Anderson were definitely that and more.

4

So much for not landing in the Unforgivably Stupid category, Noelle thought as she sat silent and seething in the front seat of the car. Christmas decorations hung from the lamp posts as they made their way through town, a series of candy canes and heralding angels hanging from their lofty perches. Tree trunks wrapped in white lights lined Main Street proper and windows dressed in evergreen and candlelight glittered in the night.

Snow didn't fall often in Mississippi, but cold was something they were all familiar with. As such, shoppers were wrapped in heavy coats and gloves, toddlers in puffy jackets of varying colors, making them look like little marshmallows with heads. The thought made her smile, which felt a bit like a betrayal considering how absolutely dumb she'd been.

The GPS in her phone. Geez, Lord, hadn't she watched enough crime dramas to know better? How many times had a victim been traced via their last cell phone activity? How many times had the bad guys been captured because they'd messed up and used one?

To be fair, she hadn't used her cell since she'd gone into protective custody—not because she'd been aware of the danger, but because she simply hadn't had anyone to call. The bulk of her correspondence had been through email and when she'd wanted to check that, she'd just used Clark's. She hadn't considered, hadn't even thought that she might be putting them all in danger. She bit the inside of her cheek, blinking back tears.

If anything happened to them because of her...

She couldn't bear to think about it. Concern and worry gnawed at her, made her want to go back and apologize for potentially risking their safety when they'd been nothing but kind to her.

And all because she'd allowed *him* to irritate her.

She peeked a withering glance in his direction, berating herself for the immediate bolt of heat that hit her middle. And honestly, she considered herself lucky that it was only a bolt of heat and not a full-fledged conflagration, like the one that had descended upon her like the legendary fires of hell the instant he'd lifted her up over his massive, powerful shoulder.

Mercy.

She'd been too stunned to react at all at first. To begin with, she wasn't accustomed to anyone picking her up at all. Not since she was a child, anyway. That he'd done it, this dark-haired giant of a man with the most mouthwatering body she'd ever laid eyes on, was nothing short of staggering. He'd lifted her easily, as though her weight and size were negligible.

Which they weren't, she knew.

At five foot eight, Noelle was tallish and had the frame to go along with her height. While she wasn't exactly overweight, if she suddenly lost ten pounds she knew she wouldn't miss it. She liked food and she liked to eat and, thankfully, she was active enough to be able to indulge herself occasionally without worry that she wouldn't be able to fit into her clothes the next day. At any rate, she was not petite, she was healthy.

But the minute she'd gone over his shoulder…she'd felt positively dainty.

And her stupid heart had skipped a beat and her stupid body had boiled with blistering awareness, settling hotly in her suddenly drenched sex. She'd tingled from head to toe, a sensation that had only intensified from her vantage point, which had put her in close proximity to his extremely well-made ass.

Pride and irritation had kept her from completely coming unglued, so she'd managed to pretend like she was merely outraged and entertained by his oafish behavior when, truthfully, she'd been unaccountably, *gallingly* thrilled. Some part of that masculine display of strength had called to her on a purely base feminine level—a throwback to prehistoric times, no doubt, when the man had to club dinner over the head and drag it home to eat. When a woman slept with a man at night to make him sleepy and prevent him from making off to another cave, to another bear skin rug.

That she'd reacted as she had was as puzzling as it was distressful.

Truthfully, she'd always considered herself above such things, had always been more attracted to an intellectual mind. Did that mean she couldn't appreciate a little eye candy? No. She could and did—*Magic Mike,* anyone?—but when it came to what really drew her, a clever sense of humor and intelligent mind were ordinarily what turned her on.

Judd Anderson had turned her on before she'd even gotten a proper look at him. More so than any other man ever. And, as a former Ranger, she knew that he was intelligent. The jury was still out on his sense of humor, but judging from his little jab about dragging her in by the hair when they got to wherever the hell it was that they were going, she imagined it leaned toward the darker side.

That fit, she thought. Between that shiny black hair and equally arrestingly black eyes, a bubbly sense of humor would be horribly out of place. Though she still hadn't managed to truly study him as she wished—he had that sort of face, the kind that drew one in and didn't let go—she knew beauty when she saw it. And he was beautiful, an adjective that would no doubt offend him.

Offensive or not, it was still true.

His skin was smooth with honeyed undertones that suggested he'd tan well, his cheeks high and the hollows beneath just sharp enough to be intriguing, but full enough to prevent being harsh. The dashboard lights illuminated his face, the passing cars giving her additional glimpses as they went by, flickering like an exhausted reel of film. The light between shadows revealed heavy-lidded eyes, a purely carnal mouth, one that was full and wide and presently set in a displeased line. The muscle in his jaw worked and tension vibrated off his massive body so thoroughly that she imagined she could see it in waves, pulsing like sonar.

He wasn't just angry, he was livid.

And it was her fault.

She wasn't exactly certain how she felt about that—she wavered between indifference and regret—but probably wouldn't have been as concerned had she not compromised her position with a mistake. And a *big* one, at that.

She wrapped her arms a little more tightly around the basket, using it like a shield, then swallowed. "Would you please check in with Les and the boys a little later, just so I'll know that they're all right?"

He didn't look at her, but merely nodded and drummed his thumb against the steering wheel.

"Would you mind telling me where we're going?" she ventured. The continued silence was starting to get to her. Hell, she knew she'd messed up. His refusing to speak to her wasn't going to flay her any more than her own conscience.

"To a new safe house."

Obviously. Irritation bubbled quickly once again and she struggled to keep it in check. She would *not* allow him to goad her. She *wouldn't.*

"I had sort of worked that bit out for myself, thanks," she said, careful to keep the sarcasm out of her voice. "Could you be more specific?"

"I could, but I won't."

Noelle felt her eyes narrow, her jaw clench. A hot retort burned up the back of her throat, but she swallowed it back, determined to move this bad-start relationship into more cordial territory. "That's—" *asinine, petty, small* "—unfortunate," she managed, nearly choking on the word.

He did look at her then and though he didn't smile, she thought she detected the barest tug on his lips. "That's not what you wanted to say, was it?"

She shifted primly in her seat and lifted her chin. "I'm trying to be pleasant," she said. That he *wasn't* was strongly implied.

"Let me know how that works out for you," he said with a grim chuckle. "I tried it earlier this evening and it backfired *spectacularly* for me."

Annoyed, Noelle opened her mouth, then clamped it shut. *Don't respond, don't respond, don't respond.* "That's odd," she remarked, a low edge to her voice that she couldn't seem to control anymore than her mouth. "I don't remember you being pleasant at all."

"Oh, I imagine it's difficult to recognize without my lips glued to your ass, like those of your previous detail, but you'll work it out soon enough."

Of all the unmitigated gall... She felt her eyebrows wing up her forehead and swiveled to face him. "You're rude."

"I'm efficient. I'm not surprised that you don't recognize the difference."

She gritted her teeth. Back to that were they? "I

wasn't made aware that you were coming for me to-night until a few minutes before you arrived," she said, her temper needle edging into the red zone once more. "Les didn't want to worry me. He was afraid that I'd be upset at having to move *yet* again. In the past three weeks I've been shot at twice, nearly burned to death once and moved to four different lo-cations. I haven't been able to go home, which is just as well," she added with a slightly manic chuckle, "since it's still uninhabitable from the fire I narrowly escaped." She glared at him. "I am *not* inefficient, you arrogant autocratic ass," she said, biting off each word. "I am tired and I am scared and I just want my damned life back." She turned and stared straight ahead, perturbed that she'd let him do it again, en-gage her in another pointless argument. Oh, well, Noelle thought. In for a penny, in for a pound. "And you can suck it."

JUDD BLINKED AND a startled laugh—one he desper-ately needed—burst from his throat. "Suck wh-what exactly?" he asked, chuckling under his breath.

He didn't have to see her eyes to know that she'd rolled them. He could hear it in her tone, in that be-leaguered, put-upon pitch. "Go to hell."

Suck it, indeed. He smiled, tsked a reproof. "I thought you were trying to be pleasant."

"It's not worth it," she said with a little arm wave. "It's either point out your idiocy or have a stroke, and I have too much self-preservation to have you kill me, particularly when you're the jackass who is supposed to be keeping me alive. Or had you forgotten?" she drawled.

Honest to God, she was the most provoking woman he'd ever met in his life. "I haven't forgotten. But considering you attempted to have me replaced within minutes of my arrival, I have to admit I've lost a bit of enthusiasm on that score."

"Enthusiasm or not, it's your job. Wounded your pride, did I?" she asked with a pointed quirk of her brow. "Had you been the least bit agreeable, I wouldn't have made the call. You weren't. You were a jerk. I didn't foresee a pleasant few days for either of us."

He didn't either, but for different reasons than she did, obviously. Even now, he was more aware of the mulish set of her ripe lips than the words coming out of them. "I wasn't a jerk—I was right. From your reaction, I can only conclude that was a novel experience for you." He glanced in the rearview mirror, keeping a close watch on the activity behind them. "I wasn't the one with wounded pride, sweetheart. That was you."

Her adorable chin jacked up another notch. "Don't

call me sweetheart. It's patronizing and I don't like it."

He laughed darkly again and shook his head in disbelief. "*I'm* patronizing? *I'm* patronizing? Oh, that's rich."

He felt that green stare bore into the side of his head and she narrowed her eyes in suspicion. "What are you talking about?"

Judd negotiated the turn that would take them to the main highway, then later onto the interstate. "You talked to me like I was an incompetent moron, then had the audacity to suggest that I'm so ignorant that I don't know the difference between men beneath my command and the rest of the world. And you have the nerve to accuse *me* of being patronizing?" he asked, his voice climbing. He grunted. "I suggest you check that definition again and then take a look in the mirror, *sweetheart*. Because you're the personification of it."

She smoothed a nonexistent wrinkle from her skirt, avoiding his gaze. "You provoke me," she said churlishly, in what he thought he was supposed to accept as an admission of guilt. "I don't like being told what to do."

He laughed again, shook his head. "Show me a person who does."

She shot him a look, a shadow of a smile on her

mouth. "Touché." A pause, then, more quietly, less angrily, "I shouldn't have used the phone."

That was probably as close to an apology for calling Payne as he was likely to get, Judd thought. He still couldn't believe that she'd done it, that she'd been so annoyed with him over that little verbal exchange—not even a good argument, dammit—that she'd called and asked for a replacement.

Yes, it had embarrassed him. This was his *first* assignment for Ranger Security, his maiden voyage, so to speak. His proving ground.

More than the humiliation, though, she was right. It *had* wounded his pride. Had she called because he'd been incompetent or made a mistake, it would have been justified. He wouldn't have liked it, but he would have accepted it. But having her call because he'd had the balls to stand up to her and point out the flaws in her reasoning smacked too much of an intentional retreat. And nothing about her—in person or on file—had suggested he'd be protecting a coward.

So why had she done it? Why had she scurried into that depressing little bedroom and called his boss? What was it about him, specifically, that she found so beyond redemption that she didn't want to spend a single unnecessary moment in his company? Especially when she'd seemed so fond of that band of happy misfits she'd spent the past two weeks with? If she could find redeeming qualities in all of them, then surely she ought to be able to find one in him as well. But she hadn't even wanted to try. Wounded pride?

Damn straight.

And it blew.

Clearly he needed to get a rubber band for his own wrist and pop it every time he was tempted to howl in frustration. Like now. Because there was no way in hell he was jealous of Les and Clark and Roy. He scowled. Especially Roy, with his curly hair and All You Can Eat Buffet body. Dammit, now he was being uncharitable. Unkind. Bitchy, even. What the hell was wrong with him? His gaze slid to her.

She was The Problem.

Noelle. So named because her birthday and Christmas were one in the same. No doubt that had sucked when she'd been a kid, Judd thought, watching as she lifted the lid to the basket and looked in on her kittens. Less trouble for her parents, but never having a dedicated day that was just about her like so many other people. Had they wrapped some of her birthday presents and put them under the tree? he wondered. Or had they simply sang "Happy Birthday" while she opened her Christmas gifts?

A little black paw darted out and a series of squeaky meows sounded in the silent cab of the SUV. She smiled then, her face softening with pleasure and affection. Her fiery hair gleamed in the light of passing cars, making it flicker like flames. It was gorgeous, that hair. Made him want to fist his hands in it and draw her to him. And since he didn't seem to have the least little bit of control where she was concerned, it wouldn't surprise him if he just snapped at some point and did just that.

Like picking her up and tossing her over his shoulder. He still couldn't recall where the idea had come from, if he'd even thought of it at all before doing it. One second he'd been seeing red, wrapped up in a haze of humiliation and anger, and the next her soft belly was on his shoulder, her softer, plump breasts against his back and her rump—the one that, in his estimation, would win the Best Ass Ever contest— was so close he could have turned his head and literally kissed it, had he wanted.

He wanted. Desperately. Violently. Beyond all reason.

And he'd known her less than an hour.

It didn't take a genius to see that this had all the hallmarks of a beautiful disaster in the making.

Honestly, when he'd first been handed her case file, he'd imagined that this assignment was going to be easy—potentially boring, even. It was the classic wrong-place-at-the-wrong time scenario. He'd whisk her off to some undisclosed but safe location and keep her there until delivering her into the care of the district attorney when her testimony was to begin. The Ranger Security wives had put together a care package for her, adding lots of books and movies—chick flicks he had no intention of watching—and plenty of girly bath products. Because she'd been through the fire, they'd also inquired after her size and included several items of clothing for her.

On the surface, Noelle Montgomery sounded like a nice girl with a good heart who'd fully embraced her humanitarian lifestyle. Her résumé of work was impressive and her financials had revealed a woman who was generous, but smart. She had no close living relatives, other than her parents, who seemed more interested in their next African safari or Alaskan cruise than their daughter or what she was doing. She seemed to move tirelessly from one disaster area to another and volunteered at local clinics and kitchens when she was between efforts.

It was almost manic, the way she flitted about and, though he suspected she generally enjoyed the work she did and that it was important to her, he almost wondered if she was so keen to be in the field because being home was too uncomfortable for her. She was driven—he couldn't deny that. But was the cause driving her or was something else? He didn't know and shouldn't care.

But, naturally, he did.

How odd, Judd thought, that he should be paired with her. While she was all goodness and light—and mouthy and infuriating—and determined to do as much as she could for her fellow man, devoted to feeding the hungry, nursing the sick and saving lives…he'd been on the other side of the world deliberately, purposely taking them.

And yet, on the surface, they'd been on the same side. Judd swallowed, his shoulders suddenly tight with tension, a knot of dread forming in his belly.

He seriously doubted she'd see it that way.

And, at the moment, when comparing her body of work to his, admittedly he had a problem seeing it as well.

There was a disturbing truth hidden in that thought, one that he shied away from examining because he grimly suspected he wouldn't care for the revelation.

Judd shook off the unpleasant sensation, focused instead on the job at hand—keeping her safe. God knew it had to be less difficult than his previous job and, whereas he'd been certain of that before, he was unhappily less confident now. Payne was right—she was going to be hard to handle…particularly considering how much he wanted to *handle* her.

5

"You caught a break. GPS monitoring got a hit. 504 Cedar," the voice on the other end of the line told him. "The clock is ticking, money man. You're a dead man walking if you screw it up again."

Click.

Hands shaking so hard he could barely get the cigarette to his lips, Curtis Hanson took a much-needed drag and released the plume of smoke with a weary, fatalistic chuckle. And the hell of it? He didn't smoke. Or at least he hadn't until a few weeks ago.

A dead man walking? Tubby's man had warned. Hell, he'd been a dead man walking the instant he'd made the stupid decision to go into business with the notorious local crime boss. Although, strictly speaking, he wasn't sure if he'd actually made a decision. Tubby had strongly suggested that if Curtis didn't clean the money for him through The Ark—the town's primary help center, funded by the collective generosity of the local churches—that he'd string him up by his balls and then make him watch as his children were tortured. He had a cousin, he'd said, who loved to play with knives, got off on hearing little girls squeal.

He shuddered now, even thinking about it.

Curtis, should he decide to "help,"—thus preventing his eight- and ten-year-old daughters from feeling the sharp edge of Tubby's crazy cousin's knife—would get a ten percent cut for his trouble, which had ultimately ended up being more than half of his regular salary at the bank.

Greed, Curtis thought now. It really was the most insidious, harmful thing. Because once Tubby had gotten his hooks into him at The Ark and given him a little taste beyond living pay check to pay check, he'd come to him with another offer, and then another, and it wasn't long until he'd gone from being a law-abiding citizen with what he'd believed was a decent moral compass…to this.

A hit man.

He laughed low and shook his head. He was a piss poor one, clearly, but then he'd never tried to kill anyone before. But it was amazing what one would do when pushed to the limit, when forced to protect one's family. And as a so-called upstanding member of the community, he was supposedly above suspicion. The only man for the job.

Simply put, it was her or them. Noelle Montgomery—whom he'd known most of her life and actually liked—or his wife and girls.

The choice, in the end, had been surprisingly easy.

The actual killing, on the other hand—or "elimination" as Tubby's people liked to say—was proving rather difficult. He'd shot at her and missed twice, and had done a bang-up job setting her house on fire, but she'd managed to escape that as well. And after that bungled attempt, Ed Johnson—his father-in-law—had stepped in and made sure that she was put into private custody. Though he'd tried to covertly wheedle Noelle's whereabouts from him, Ed had revealed that he didn't know and didn't want to know. All he'd said was that she was in the best hands money could buy—and he ought to know since he had so much of it—and that she'd be safe until the trial.

If that was the case, then his father-in-law had inadvertently helped put the final nail in his coffin, most likely making a widow out of his daughter.

It was a funny old world, wasn't it?

He ground the cigarette into the smokeless ashtray hidden in his desk drawer, fired a little freshener into the air and then popped a breath mint into his mouth. Carla, his wife, hated his new habit and would flip if she suspected he'd been smoking. But this was his office—his sanctuary—the only room in the whole damned house that was truly his and he'd decided that, in this instance, he was going to do as he damned well pleased.

Time to move. *Tick, tock, tick, tock...*

He picked up his keys and cell phone from his desk, then strolled calmly down the hall. His daughters, Caro and Breanne, were sprawled on opposite ends of the couch watching the Disney channel as he walked by. He paused, spying the box of cheesy snacks on the coffee table.

"Don't ruin your dinner," he admonished. "You know you're not supposed to have snacks past four."

Breanne, his youngest smiled, revealing a large gap where her two front teeth used to be. She'd pulled them herself, then insisted that they pay her for her trouble and let her keep her teeth instead of giving them to the tooth fairy. "We're not eating them anymore," she said. "Just looking at the box," she sighed, "remembering how good they taste."

Caro giggled, darting him a look. "She's such a dork."

"Hey," he said, trying to summon a frown. "She's not a dork. She's just got a flair for the dramatic."

Bre lifted a brow. "Are you going somewhere, Daddy?" She bounded up onto her knees, her expression hopeful. "Can I go with you?"

His heart squeezed and nausea swirled in his belly. "Not today, sweetheart. I've got to run down to The Ark for a few minutes. I won't be gone long."

Her face fell. "Promise?"

"I promise."

He found Carla in the kitchen, stirring a pot of pasta sauce and repeated The Ark excuse. He hated lying to her, hated even more that he'd gotten so good at it.

She frowned. "You'll be back in time for dinner?"

"Barring any unforeseen complication, yes," he said. Like being arrested for attempted murder. 504 Cedar, he reminded himself.

It was now or never.

He breathed in the scent of marinara, let his gaze skim along the sweet curve of his wife's cheek, listened to his daughters laughing from the other room. Took a mental snapshot of everything he'd taken for granted. Everything he'd put in jeopardy. Regret washed through him, but it didn't lessen the sting.

Quitting, unfortunately, wasn't an option. Not for him. Not anymore.

"The company has a safe house just a little north of Ellijay," he said, his smooth voice less confrontational than before, glancing once again at the rear-view mirror.

He was constantly checking it and everything else around them, looking for followers, she assumed. Given how he'd noted the makes and models of the cars on the street of the previous house, she was certain if she quizzed him right now, he'd be able to do same.

That was impressive, she'd admit.

Additionally, while she was certain that he wasn't always looking at her—he couldn't and still drive properly—she was nevertheless sure that he knew every move she made, was aware of each breath she took and which direction she released it.

It was as unnerving as it was thrilling. There was something undeniably attractive about that level of attention to detail. Knowing that he didn't—or wouldn't—miss anything. And if he was this committed to that sort of awareness, then logic demanded he'd take that singular, focused approach to *everything*. Concentrated, determined, thorough. The thought made her belly tighten, the backs of her knees tingle.

"Thank you," she said. "It's a little thing, knowing where one is going, but it helps."

He was quiet for a moment. "It's roughly a five-hour drive. It'll be late when we get there, but I'd rather push on through if you're up to it. The sooner we're on site, the sooner we'll be able to lock things down and relax."

Noelle didn't anticipate being able to do much relaxing—just the opposite in fact, with him around—but refrained from commenting. What could she say, really, that wouldn't sound argumentative or reveal too much? Like how her womb was steaming with heat, anticipating a release that wasn't going to arrive in the near future. He was merely supposed to *guard* her body, not service it. And since he didn't seem to particularly like her, it begged a lot of wishful thinking to even entertain the idea that he'd be interested in doing anything with her beyond his job.

Hell, for all she knew he might even have a girlfriend—a vicious twist of envy gripped her at the thought—or a fiancée. She'd noted the absence of a ring on his left hand, so she presumed he wasn't married. Naturally, that begged the question why. Why had someone so smart and lethally handsome not married a supermodel brainiac and produced lots of brilliant, beautiful children? Had the career gotten in the way? Or was it something else? Was he merely a confirmed bachelor who enjoyed his freedom?

On a personal level, while Noelle had always imagined that she'd settle down and marry and have a family of her own, the reality of that ever happening was getting slimmer and slimmer. She inwardly rolled her eyes. Unfortunately, she'd yet to find a man she'd want to spend more than a few evenings with, much less marry. She wanted the Big Romance. She wanted to be swept off her feet, fall head over heels in love with someone who thought she hadn't just hung the moon, but all the other stars and planets as well. She wanted to be adored. She wanted her quirks to be endearing, her bed head sexy, her bad moods forgotten and forgiven. She grinned.

And if he had an excellent sense of humor, a keen mind, an appreciation of honor and happened to be drop dead gorgeous, then all the better.

The first three requirements were non-negotiable, but the last she was willing to compromise on. After all, a girl didn't have to have everything and she wasn't so shallow that she was incapable of appreciating a deeper, inner beauty. In her opinion, some of life's truest treasures could be found beneath the surface. Her gaze strayed to the basket in her lap.

Like her kittens.

She strongly suspected that the pair had been dumped by some superstitious fool who hadn't looked beyond their black fur and curious condition, had only seen a bad omen and lots of vet bills.

She, on the other hand, had.

And the bond that she'd formed with the pair was

special, whether it was borne out of the horror of seeing the murder or from knowing that she'd been the perfect person to rescue them, she'd never know. Probably a combination of both. But it was there all the same. An undeniable connection.

Because she traveled so much and so often, Noelle had always refrained from having pets. It wasn't fair to take on an animal, make it dependent upon you and allow it to develop an attachment, and then leave it in the care of someone else. And because pets were usually the forgotten victims of natural disasters, she'd always made it a point to forge good relationships with reputable, no-kill shelters. When she came across animals in need—and she often did— she'd do the rescue and then hand them off, certain of their proper care and eventual adoption.

But with the kittens she hadn't been able to do that. She hadn't been able to part with them. Not because she suspected they'd get any sort of ill treatment or wouldn't find a home, but because they were *hers*. Doing the drop-off with an abused animal or cute puppy or cat had never been easy, but she'd still been able to make the break. With Lilo and Stitch, she'd made the arrangements, but then had called back and cancelled. When she'd said she was going to keep them—when those words had come out of her mouth—no one could have been any more surprised than she'd been.

But there it was.

She had absolutely no plan as to what she'd do with them, who would care for them, the next time she had to leave, but she'd simply have to figure something out. She was theirs and they were hers. The end. And considering she had the trial to get through first, then the renovation of her house post-fire, she knew that she wouldn't have to worry about it for a while. She'd never appreciated Scarleyt O'Hara's I'll-think-about-that-tomorrow approach—the absence of a plan made her twitchy—but in this case, she was simply going to have to make an exception. Break her own rule, as it were.

To her chagrin, her stomach suddenly rumbled loudly, echoing like gunfire into the silence. From the corner of her eye, she watched Judd's lips twitch, the barest hint of what a genuine smile might look like on his face and her traitorous body responded accordingly, heating anew.

"I take it you haven't eaten," he said, his twinkling gaze swinging briefly to hers, the impact devastatingly intimate despite its brevity.

She shook her head. "Dinner was in the oven. I hope someone remembers to take it out," she said absently, suddenly worried about the potential waste.

He laughed. "They're men. They'll remember there's a home-cooked meal available." He passed another car, smoothly sliding into the space in front of it. She liked the way he drove, unhurried, but confident. "Meat loaf, right?"

She nodded, surprised. "It was. My grandmother's recipe."

Her grandmother had been all about comfort food and had shared her passion with Noelle. Which was good, because if she'd waited on her mother to teach her how to cook she'd have never learned. Her mother had been a firm believer in take-out and the microwave and used to joke that she could barely boil water. Domestic things had never been her strong suit, probably because she hadn't really cared about them. She'd been devoted to her job as the editor of their local paper and to Noelle's father. Anything else had been secondary.

Including Noelle.

Her mother had once confided that they'd never planned on having children, that she'd been a "happy surprise." She wasn't entirely sold on the "happy" bit, but she didn't doubt that she was a surprise. And she'd been loved, too. She knew that. In as much as two mutually devoted to each other, self-absorbed people could be, anyway. Thankfully, she'd had her grandparents to fill the gap, and there wasn't a day that went by when she didn't miss them, when she didn't think about them. Stupid cancer...

"It smelled good," he remarked. "I noticed it when I came in."

"There was plenty. Pity we didn't have time to stick around and eat it," she couldn't help but needle. "I'd made a pie as well. But with a five-hour drive ahead of us, I suppose going through a drive-thru is the best option." Better to end on a conciliatory note, she decided. She'd made her point.

A low bark of laughter tumbled up his throat and he shook his head, a smile on his lips. "You just can't help yourself, can you?"

She blinked innocently, though she knew exactly what he was talking about. "I'm sorry?"

"No, you're not," he said, seemingly mystified. He chuckled darkly. "You are lots of things, but 'sorry' isn't one of them."

She didn't know if she liked the sound of that. What did he mean by "lots of things"? Good things, bad things? It was so ambiguous and, despite his tone, she couldn't get a true bead on the meaning behind it.

"The most important thing I am right now is hungry," she remarked matter-of-factly, the back of her neck prickling as she watched him negotiate another lane change. His hands were large and long-fingered, capable at the wheel. Capable of lots of other tasks as well, she imagined. The thought of them sliding along her jaw suddenly materialized in her mind's eye, making a shudder stream through her.

"Yes, I heard," he drawled, darting her another sidelong glance. "There's an energy bar in the console to tide you over," he said, gesturing to the space between them. "We'll stop in the next town."

"I can't eat an energy bar without something to drink," she said. "I'll choke. I have a strong gag reflex." Good Lord, had she really said that aloud? Mortification stung her cheeks and she inwardly winced, horrified. The silence in the cab suddenly swelled with tension, one of those awful pregnant pauses that seemed to lengthen impossibly with every second that rolled by.

He chewed the inside of his cheek. Hesitated. Cleared his throat, presumably of a laugh. "I'll be sure to keep that in mind."

6

SOPHOMORIC OR GUTTER-BRAINED, call it whatever you want, but typically when a man heard the words "gag reflex"—much like those association card games shrink's liked to use—his first thought was "blow job."

Butter—biscuit.

Peanut butter—jelly.

Gag reflex—blow job.

It was just the way most men were wired and, though he liked to consider himself a little more evolved than most men—certainly above the curve, at any rate—evidently he was not.

Because when she'd said gag reflex, he'd immediately imagined her lovely raspberry bow-like mouth wrapped around his dick, her fiery hair spread out over his bare thighs, and the resulting image had made him harden past the point of pain, made his hands involuntarily tighten on the wheel. The only thing that prevented him from shifting into a more comfortable position was the fact that he knew she would notice—despite the high color on her peachy cheeks—and, more importantly, the she-devil would know *why* he'd moved and then she'd have even *more* power over him.

She already, after less than an hour in her company, had him turned upside down and inside out. The idea that she could potentially have him eating out of her hand the same way she'd had those mindless pups back at the safe house doing it was just enough incentive to keep him in check.

He would *not* allow it.

He couldn't afford to be that reckless, not when her life and his future at Ranger Security hung in the balance. Naturally, her life was more important—he could get another job if he needed to—but he sure as hell didn't want to have to seek alternate employment.

I am a professional, Judd told himself. *An adult. The ultimate master of my actions.*

Evidently hungry enough to risk choking, she shifted in the darkness, then turned to open the console. Her bare fingers brushed his arm in the process, shocking him with a crackle of static. He gritted his teeth, feeling the jolt rush through his balls.

She jumped a little and quickly withdrew her hand. "Sorry."

"There's a case of water in the back," he said. "It hasn't been refrigerated, but it sat in the truck overnight, so it should be cold enough."

"Thanks," she said. "I'd better get a bottle." She adjusted her seat so that she could put her basket onto the floor, then unhooked her safety belt and scrambled between the two seats, her lush rump narrowly missing his head as she wriggled past.

He wasn't going to survive this, Judd thought, every muscle in his body going taut. Not with a shred of sanity or the enamel on his teeth. By the time he delivered her for trial, he'd be a blathering idiot with newly groomed hair. Which reminded him...

"I didn't realize that you were a hairdresser," he said. "Your file simply said humanitarian."

His gaze drifted to the rearview mirror—an apt description, considering her rump was all he could see—and her muffled voice reached him from the back. "I'm not a hairdresser," she said. She tore into the plastic, cursing under her breath when it didn't cooperate as quickly as she'd like.

"Then why were you giving Roy a haircut?"

She grunted in victory. "Do you want one, too? While I'm back here?"

Might as well. His mouth was as dry as a desert at the moment, anyway. "Yes, thanks."

"Just because I haven't been formally trained doesn't mean I don't know how to give a basic trim, which was all I was doing." She came forward again, stuck a bare leg through the two front seats, then withdrew it. "Well, hell. This is going to be a little trickier than I thought."

Right, Judd thought, his mouth curving. Evidently going to the back had been easier than coming to the front. Her predicament was endlessly entertaining. Which was a little pathetic, when he thought about it. So he didn't.

"Were Roy and the others aware of your limited experience before they turned you loose with a pair of scissors?"

She grunted, made another awkward attempt to come through, this time head first—it didn't work. "I don't remember," she said. "But it wouldn't have mattered. They trusted me."

He hummed under his breath. "Blindly, it would seem."

"This is...I—" She wiggled around a little more, putting both feet forward this time, nearly knocking the car out of gear in the process. "Oh, hell. Sorry," she muttered sheepishly.

"That's not going to work," he said. "Unless you

can magically grow longer arms to give you the needed leverage to come through."

"Yes, I'd worked that bit out for myself, thanks," she said tightly, seemingly annoyed with herself.

"Put both feet on the floor board and stand up."

"I'm too tall to stand up."

"Obviously. Crouch," he told her.

She heaved an exasperated breath, shoved the hair out of her face. "If you're going to start bossing me around again, we're going to have a problem. Honestly, do you even hear yourself? *Put both feet on the floor. Stand up. Crouch,*" she mimicked. "It's irritating."

"I'm trying to be helpful," he told her, feeling his own temper rise. "But never mind. I'm sure you can work it out on your own."

"Yes, I'm sure I can," she said, her tone smug enough to make him want to scream. He floored it instead, gunning the motor as he passed another car, and sent her tumbling backward, landing with an "oomph" and a grunt on her rear end.

"That was juvenile."

He turned his head to hide his smile. "I don't have any idea what you're talking about."

"Liar." She scooted forward and stood, crouching low. "Fine, I'll try it your way. What next, Boy Genius?"

"Boy Genius, my hero, Arrogant Autocratic Ass," he listed off. "I'm not opposed to a nickname, per se, if you're going to give me one, but I have to say I don't care for any of my choices thus far. I am not a boy," he said, biting the words off. "Nor am I a hero. And while I *am* confident, I'm not arrogant." He released a breath. "Someone needs to get you a dictionary for Christmas."

He darted a look in the mirror just in time to see a shadow race over her features, one that tugged at him, made him feel like he'd said something unintentionally hurtful.

She rallied quickly, though, making him wonder if he'd imagined the look. "That still makes you an autocratic ass," she said.

"Here's a thought," he said. "Why don't you just call me by my name? Judd. Simple enough. One syllable. Or 'Judd the Heroic Confident Genius?' if you want to combine the remains of the others?"

"Judd the Heroic Confident Genius?" she said, humor shaking her voice. "Wow," she said, shaking her head. "Just wow. " A little pause, then, "Are you really a genius?" she asked suspiciously, almost like she dreaded the answer. Her tone made him grin.

He was. "Profoundly gifted" according to his test scores. "What do you think?" he asked, genuinely curious.

She sighed heavily, relaxed against the backseat and opened the water bottle. "Probably so," she said, sounding dejected. She grimaced. "It would be my luck."

Judd chuckled low, looking at her thoughtful, glum expression. He didn't have any idea what to make of her response, but for reasons which escaped him, it cheered him all the same.

"My grandfather was a barber," she announced from the backseat, picking up their conversation pre-argument, as though it had never happened. "I had no formal training, but I spent a lot of time at his shop." She met his gaze in the mirror, that lovely, startling green tangling with his. "That's where I learned to do a decent trim and shave."

"Oh." That was one question answered, Judd thought. Naturally—stupidly—he had thousands more. She was too intriguing by half and he was too curious for comfort.

Maybe she'd had the right of it to start, he thought. Maybe a different agent would have been better suited to this task. One that had a better grasp on his control and his tongue. One that could look at her and not think about sliding his *controlled tongue* down the length of her luscious body.

Because he sure as hell couldn't.

THEY'D JUST STOPPED to let Lilo and Stitch out for a quick romp in the grass and to pee in the sandy gravel by the roadside when Noelle noticed that Judd had evidently received a text and, judging from his dark expression, the news it contained wasn't good.

She carefully reeled the kittens in on their leashes, smiling when Lilo batted at Stitch's tail and made her way over to where he stood, the kittens tangling around her ankles. He'd leaned against the hood of the SUV, a booted foot against the bumper as he broodingly watched her approach. Another pitch of desire hummed through her. Mercy, he was hot. "You can leave them out of the basket if you can keep them from darting up under my feet while I'm driving," he said, eyeing her pets.

"I'd rather not risk it," she said. "They're small and devilishly quick. And even if I could keep them from getting under your feet, there's no guarantee I couldn't keep them from climbing all over your head. It's better this way. They actually like the basket, so that makes things easier." She frowned, tucked a strand of hair away from her face. "What's wrong?" she asked, glancing at the phone still in his hand.

He looked at her, his dark eyes even blacker under the evening sky. "What makes you think anything is wrong?"

She felt her lips twitch. "The thunderclouds rolling across your face."

"Jeb always said I was easy to read," he remarked quietly, more to himself than to her. "Unlike him," he grunted. "Mr. Mysterious."

"Jeb?" Who was this Jeb? If it was his boyfriend, then she'd save her attackers a bullet and shoot herself. Because that would be unforgivably unfair. Cruel, even.

"My brother," he said. "My twin."

She felt her eyes widen in shock. "Twin? There are two of you?" she asked, her voice rising. Two of *him?* Loose on the population at large, free to wreak havoc with female hormones at will? Good Lord... Well, that was certainly proof that the Almighty had a sense of humor.

He laughed, revealing a deep dimple in his left cheek. She smothered a whimper. Criminally handsome, magnificently built, sexy as hell. Her cheeks puffed as she exhaled mightily. And *dimples*.

She was doomed, Noelle thought, feeling that tell-tale dip and clench deep in her belly. Doomed, doomed, doomed.

"We're not identical," he said. "Exact opposites, as it happens. Jeb is a blue-eyed blonde. Rather angelic-looking I'm told." The corner of his lip curled significantly. "I am not."

A shuddering breath left her lungs. No, he wasn't. He was strikingly dark, that black hair and blacker eyes contrasting vividly with his gorgeous skin. The parking lot lights glowed brightly from above, giving him a strangely ethereal quality, and her gaze inexplicably dropped to his mouth.

Curved just so, it had a devastating effect on her equilibrium and seemed to knock her off balance and forward, closer to him. The cold air suddenly crackled with a new tense heat, sizzling along her nerve endings. Longing welled up inside of her, so fierce and so quickly that she nearly groaned aloud, giving voice to the need hammering through her.

His black as sin gaze dropped to her mouth, lingered hungrily, before returning to her eyes and the raw desire she saw staring back at her nearly ripped the breath from her seizing lungs. He looked away, swallowed, then pushed off from the car and put some much needed distance between them.

He obviously had more strength of will than she did.

"That was my boss," he said.

She blinked. "What?"

"You asked if something was wrong," he reminded her. "I got a text from my boss. The Cedar Street safe house went up in flames a few minutes ago. Another Molotov cocktail, this one more potent than the last."

She sucked in a breath, horror billowing through her. "What? The boys? Roy? Les? Clark?"

"They're all safe," he assured her. "They'd left immediately following us."

She wilted with relief, her body weary after the post-adrenaline rush brought on by fear. Noelle felt tears prick the backs of her lids and resisted the urge to scream in frustration. She was so damned tired of being afraid, of feeling powerless to keep those around her safe, much less herself.

"I want you to call D.A. Jeffrey Stark," she said, her voice cracking with anger, "and tell him that if he doesn't put a stop to this—if he doesn't make finding this miserable bastard priority number one—then I'm not going to testify. I won't do it."

He leveled a look at her, his gaze serious, his mouth set in a grim line. "You don't mean that."

It was true, she didn't . But… She lifted her chin, returned his stare. "How do you know that?" she asked, still simmering with equal levels of irritation and anger. "You don't know me. You don't know anything about me. You've looked over a file, made a few deductions and have decided you have the measure of me. Well, you don't. Any more than I do you."

An odd expression slid fleetingly over his face, a haunted shadow of…what? Relief, maybe? "That might be true," he conceded. "I don't *know* you. But

I can make a few educated guesses about your character based on the 'actions' I read in your file. In my experience, you can tell a lot more about what a person does than what they say."

Hers, too. Actions did speak louder than words. But if that was the case, then what did this madman's actions say about him? Other than he was determined to see her dead. Better still, why had Tubby killed Rupert? In the grand scheme of things, what difference did it really make if Rupert preferred one ketchup brand to another and chose to stock the one *he* liked? It was his damned café, after all. Talk about a stupid reason to kill someone.

It was evil. Pure evil.

And the most unnerving part in all of this? Mossy Ridge was a relatively small community. In all probability, the person who was trying to send her to an early grave—at the bidding of Tubby Winchester—was more than likely someone she knew, possibly even held in high regard. Because Tubby hadn't gotten to his level of organized crime without greasing a few well-connected palms.

D.A. Stark had intimated more than once that Tubby was getting help from some friends in high places. And the friends in high places were especially dangerous, because unlike Tubby—who didn't pretend to be a good guy—these men did.

Which made them all the more protective of their reputations, and gave them a whole lot more to lose.

This was what she was dealing with. *This* was why she was so afraid.

Her eyes stung once more, imagining the house up in flames, her friends trapped inside. Had she dawdled a little bit longer, they *all* could have been dead, Judd included.

She pulled in a shallow breath. "Can I have my cell phone, please?"

Judd winced. "You know I can't—"

"I'm not going to use it," she said. "I want to make sure that it's off and that no one can ever use it again." *Most especially me,* she thought feeling like the biggest idiot in the northern hemisphere. Why had she placed that call? Why the hell hadn't she stopped to think?

It would be so easy to blame him, she thought, shooting a look at Judd. Easy...but unfair. She'd snapped and retaliated, hoping to get him replaced because she didn't trust herself around him. She could hardly fault him for that. That unfortunate insight was hers and hers alone.

"I can pop off the battery," he said. "You don't have to destroy it."

"I know I don't have to, but I want to."

She thought she caught the barest glimmer of a

smile cross his lips. He sighed. "What purpose is that going to serve, really?"

She raised her chin. "It'll make me feel better."

"Fine," he said, withdrawing it from his pocket. He reluctantly handed it over. "I hope you have all your contacts saved."

"The ones I care about are memorized." She dropped it onto the ground, then stomped on it until the glass shattered and the back casing broke away from the rest of the housing. With every determined strike of her heel, she felt a little better, a little more in control. Which was probably ludicrous because to any onlooker, she no doubt looked like she'd lost her mind. But...there was something very cathartic about the process. In breaking what they'd used to track her. Like a damned animal.

"All of them?" he asked. "You've memorized all of your contacts?"

She reared back and gave the phone one more vicious kick, sending it skidding across the parking lot. Lilo and Stitch, naturally, thought this was a game and tried to take off after the pieces. "Numbers are easy. I rarely forget them."

"Really?" he asked, seemingly impressed. "How many did you have stored?"

She shrugged. "I don't know. A couple hundred, I guess."

He stilled, seemingly shocked. "And you knew *all* of them?"

She felt a blush crawl over her cheeks. "I know I'm a freak," she said. "Ask me to recite the preamble to the Declaration of Independence and I draw a blank. Ask me the bar code on top of the receipt from our dinner and I can give it to you backward." She gave her head a shake. "Weird, right?"

"I didn't even know there was a bar code on the top of our receipt," he said, smiling at her. "Wow. That's cool."

"It's not the least bit useful, but thank you, anyway."

His gaze turned a bit speculative, made her a little nervous. "I bet you're good at cards."

She was, actually. She grinned. "Vegas is in the wrong direction," she told him. "We're headed to Georgia, remember?"

He still looked hopeful, his eyes alight with the possibility of poker chips and free booze. "Maybe so, but Tunica is just a hop, skip and a jump away."

"I know," she said. She scowled significantly. "Tubby runs buses back and forth twice a day. I'd be spotted the minute we got into town."

He passed a hand over his jaw, grimaced. "Damn."

She released a disbelieving breath, feeling her eyes round. "You were really considering it, weren't you?"

"It's as good a place as any to disappear. Or it would have been, had the man who wants to see you dead not been an issue."

She chewed the inside of her cheek. "There is that."

"I wouldn't have really done it," he told her. "Just thought about it for a minute. Just like you thought about calling the D.A. and threatening not to testify," he pointed out, a shrewd glint in his dark gaze.

He had her there, the wretch. "Who says I'm still not going to do it?"

"Intuition," Judd told her. "You're scared, Noelle. I know that. You'd be a fool not to be." His voice was low, kind and laced with an understanding that surpassed good instincts. He hesitated, studying her intently with more scrutiny than she was particularly comfortable with. She felt stripped, oddly vulnerable. Her secrets open to him. "But you can be afraid without being a coward. And you're not a coward." He flashed a grin. "At least not on paper, anyway."

Ah, she thought, inclining her head. Her file. What else had he read into her? Noelle wondered. What else had he seen in her file that made him so certain he could judge her accurately? And if he'd picked up on that from whatever information his company had gleaned about her, then what would he see in her in person?

For whatever reason, her own intuition told her that he didn't—or wouldn't—miss much. And if she had a prayer of keeping any part of herself hidden or secret, then she'd better have a care.

Or she'd be in danger of caring too much.

7

JUDD MADE THE final turn onto Bear Track Road and checked the mailboxes against the house number he'd be given.

Having dozed off fifty miles ago, Noelle stretched in the seat beside him. "Are we there yet?" she teased with a chuckle, her sleepy voice low and foggy.

He grinned. "I wondered when you would ask."

"Because I've behaved like a child?" she asked. "Or because of my naturally charming sense of curiosity?"

A little of both to be honest, but he had no intention of telling her that. He'd rather enjoyed her temper tantrum in the parking lot when she'd stomped all over her phone. And he even understood it, to a point. Her world was spinning out of control, her life was in danger—and the lives of those around her, as well—and sometimes the need to just lose it, to simply say "let the chips fall where they may," was almost too powerful to resist.

But she had resisted, which had necessitated the bucket-kicking fit.

Hell, he ought to recognize one, Judd thought with an inward grin. He'd had his fair share of them as well. He cast her a droll glance. "Definitely your curiosity," he told her.

Her pale green eyes twinkled in the darkness. "*Charming* curiosity," she corrected. She frowned, her brow wrinkling in thought as she peered out through the window. "You leave that bit off and I just sound nosy."

He smothered a laugh. "Aren't you?"

"Of course not. Oh, look at that," she exclaimed, pointing to a darkened car on the side of the road with a handmade neon sign on the back windshield that read, "We're fine, thanks for asking."

Judd chuckled and shook his head.

"How odd," she remarked, sitting a little more straightly in her seat. "Are they being sarcastic or are they really stranded?"

And she thought she wasn't nosy? His lips twitched. "I don't know." Admittedly, it was bizarre.

"I think we should check on them," she said,

straining to look over her shoulder. "Turn around and go back."

"That sounded like an order. Were you ever in the military?"

"Come on, Judd. What if something is wrong?"

"I seriously doubt anything is wrong," he said, angling the car into a nearby driveway so that he could double back. Not because she'd told him to, but because his father had always taught him to never pass a motorist in distress. "If nothing else, they still have their sense of humor."

"It's—" she checked the review display "—thirty-four degrees. It's too cold to sit in a broken-down car on the side of the road."

"I didn't see anybody in the car."

"I didn't either, but that doesn't mean they're not there."

He approached slowly, turning his high beams on to get a better look into the darkened car. Two people. Early twenties. One male, behind the wheel. A female in the passenger seat. She was smiling. The driver, however, was not. He didn't see anyone in the backseat, but knew better than to assume no one was there.

"I'm going to pull alongside them and roll down my window," he told her. This felt odd. Not dangerous, necessarily, but a little off all the same. "Let me do the talking. Please," he tacked on, before she could respond. He shot her a look. "You're in hiding, remember? You can't slip up and tell anyone your name, no matter how innocent they might seem."

Her expression blanked as though the idea had never occurred to her. "Oh. Right."

Confident that she'd follow direction, Judd did as he said and slowly approached the silent car. He powered the driver's-side window down and waited for the boy opposite to do the same. He did, so the battery wasn't an issue.

"You need some help?" Judd asked him.

The girl in the seat next to him bounced delightedly up and down and punched the driver on the arm. "See!" she said. "I told you. I told you that people would stop."

The driver pulled a long-suffering breath through his nose, directed his attention at Judd. "No, thanks. We're fine. Just conducting a little social experiment, that's all."

He heard Noelle lean forward, felt her shoulder up against his. "A social experiment? What kind of social experiment?"

Judd turned to glare at her and she blinked innocently back at him.

The girl in the car answered before the boy could. "Chad is convinced that the human race is doomed because of indifference, that people simply don't care about each other anymore." She preened. "I, on the other hand, don't agree, so we staged this little experiment to see who was right. We've been sitting here for hours, pretending to be stranded, counting the cars that passed without stopping as a vote for his opinion and the cars that do as a vote for mine. Y'all passed, but you came back. That's why he's annoyed. Because I've won."

Judd didn't know whether to applaud their ingenuity or rip them a new one for wasting people's time and putting themselves in danger. Purposely luring strangers was stupid no matter which way you sliced it. Who knew who might have come along? Who knew whether an ax murderer might have decided that they were easy pickings?

"That's excellent that you've had more offers of help than not," Noelle remarked, her voice on the high end of strained. She'd moved closer to him, to keep from having to shout, he imagined, but the reason hardly mattered. Her soft breast rested against his arm and the smell of her shampoo invaded his nostrils—something fruity and warm—and a bolt of sensation landed fully in his groin. He gritted his teeth.

"But the next time you do one of these little experiments," she continued, "you should consider doing it in a safer environment—" she frowned "—sorry, I didn't catch your name."

"Marissa," the girl supplied, looking mildly chagrined.

"What a lovely name," Noelle remarked, beaming at her. She might as well climb into his lap, Judd thought. His dick couldn't get any harder. "Anyway, you should do it somewhere less secluded, Marissa. Somewhere with street lamps and excess traffic. It's far too dangerous to be out here. Better safe than sorry, right?"

Marissa glared at her partner and punched him on the arm. "See, I told you," she grumbled. "That's what I'd said," she told Noelle, as if Judd was not there at all and not part of the conversation, which he wasn't at this point. "But Chad said that people would stop when it was presumably safe, that the test wouldn't be accurate unless we moved to somewhere less desirable."

Then Chad was a moron, Judd thought. Or he'd just been looking for a place to go parking with his girlfriend, which was more likely. The boy looked at Judd, the tops of his ears pinkening with embarrassment.

Noelle chuckled and sent a knowing look at Chad. "It's possible, I suppose," she said. "But I suspect

Chad was more interested in privacy than leveling your variables."

Marissa blinked, seemingly confused. "What? But I—"

"Has he told you any ghost stories?" Noelle asked, humor lacing her voice. "Tried to scare you so that you'd snuggle up a little closer to him?" What a wonderful idea, Judd thought. He wondered if that would work on her.

Marissa's eyes widened and she inhaled audibly, then her outraged but clearly flattered gaze swung to Chad. "You opportunistic jerk!" she admonished, punching him once again. "I can't believe you—"

"Take it off the side of the road, guys," Judd told them, laughing softly under his breath. "Or into a parking lot, at the very least."

Noelle waved goodbye, then moved back over into her seat. She shook her head and chuckled, the sound soft and strangely intimate. "I'm a glass half full kind of girl and have seen the evidence of genuine human kindness, but I sincerely hope I was never—and will never—be that naive."

Judd laughed, wheeled the SUV back around and aimed it toward their cabin. Bare branches crowded the space above the road, then suddenly gave way to a low, one-lane bridge over a decent-sized creek. No doubt that water was colder than a witch's tit in a brass bra, Judd thought, glad that he lived in an era of modern convenience, the invention of the water heater being one of his favorites. "She's young," he said. "It comes with the territory."

"Or maybe she was willfully stupid," Noelle remarked thoughtfully. "Maybe she wanted a secluded spot with Chad as well, and was too afraid of potential rejection to admit it."

Hmm. Voice of experience? Judd wondered. She wasn't married, he knew, and her Facebook profile— which had been included with her file, thanks to their resident hacker, Charlie Martin—had her relationship status as "single." Had there been a recent significant other? Had someone broken her heart? Was she too wed to her causes to consider a permanent relationship? Or was it something simpler? His lips twitched.

Like not being told what to do.

Because she clearly *hated* that.

"I thought I asked you to let me do the talking," he reminded her. Smiling, he heaved a why-do-I-bother sigh, then drummed his fingers against the steering wheel. "Do you always have this sort of trouble following instruction, or is it just me you object to listening to?"

"I listened," she told him, her lips curving. "I didn't tell them my name."

He snorted. "You didn't listen. You ignored and improvised. That's not the same thing."

She turned to study him, her speculative gaze entirely too bold for comfort. "I bet they don't like that sort of initiative in the military, do they? I bet that was especially difficult for you. You don't strike me as the blind obedience type, either."

Ha. She had *no* idea. He laughed darkly. "It's not called initiative in the military, sweetheart. It's called insubordination."

And yes, blind obedience—otherwise known as the chain of command—had been unbelievably difficult for him. Yes, he'd understood the reasoning behind it. The last thing Uncle Sam needed was a group of well-trained, armed-to-the-teeth anarchists. *Someone* had to be in charge, the chief to Indian ratio kept in check. Still, the bit had chafed and he'd struggled with it from the beginning.

Jeb had known it, of course—just like everything else—but, as far as he knew, no one else ever had. That she'd picked up on that little characteristic in such a short amount of time with even less information was more than mildly disturbing. It unnerved the hell out of him. Judd didn't have any desire to be mysterious, but having one person in his life who was always in his head was enough, thank you very much. He wasn't too keen on having another. And yet…

He couldn't deny that there was a certain attractive element to it as well, something that made him feel…less alone. Which was ridiculous because he'd never been lonely, never desired a deeper connection with anyone else before—particularly a woman, after the Heather debacle. He inwardly grimaced. Interestingly enough, until now, he'd never considered just how much he'd allowed that experience to impact his life, to shape his perceptions and resulting actions.

He shied away from the rest of that thought because he gloomily suspected he wasn't going to care for the outcome of that bit of self-examination. The idea that he'd let that conniving little gold digger control him in any way beyond the breakup made him want to howl….

"Do you call everyone sweetheart or I am just special?" Noelle asked, giving her shoulders a mocking little squeeze.

Judd grinned, shook his head. "Oh, you're special, all right." Truer words, he was sure, had never been spoken. Intuition told him she was going to be particularly unique, that he was hovering on the edge of a whole new world, one that he wasn't completely sure he wanted to inhabit. "A special pain in the ass," he added under his breath.

Another truth.

"What was that?"

"Nothing," he lied. He wheeled the car into the driveway, catching the front of their cabin in the headlights in the process. "We're here," he announced, shifting the gear into Park.

Let the fun begin.

"DID YOU change your mind about dragging me in by the hair of my head?" she asked, smiling as she sent him a sidelong glance. The night was quiet and still, and a cold wind billowed up beneath her skirt, making her shiver as they neared the front porch. Thankfully, a motion light blinked on as they ascended the steps.

He sighed, the sound humorous but weary. Driving for any length of time always wore her out, so she could sympathize. "Too tired," he said. "Maybe tomorrow. You're not disappointed, are you?" he teased.

"Not in the least." Though if he wanted to pick her up and carry her again, she wouldn't have any objection. Ridiculous, Noelle thought. She was going to get her Girl Power card revoked if she didn't quit thinking about that.

Weary, but uncomfortably aware that she was going to be sleeping in the same space with this criminally sexy man—six and half feet of pure, sinful temptation—Noelle waited as patiently as possible for Judd to unlock the door and usher her in.

She caught a whiff of his cologne as she walked past, something dark with a hint of patchouli. She'd noticed it when she'd been slung over his shoulder and then later, when they'd been in the car.

It smelled better up close, enhanced by the warmth of his skin.

A zing of heat pinged her sex, sent a wave of gooseflesh up over her belly. The strength in her neck lessened beneath the weight of desire while the rest of her muscles tensed with anticipation. She inwardly winced.

They were doomed to disappointment.

Because sex, she was relatively certain, was not on the agenda.

Only she wasn't so certain that the owners of the cabin were aware of that. Because a "Welcome, Honeymooners!" banner hung from the second-story rail, and a bottle of champagne chilled in a bucket on the bar along with a basket of chocolates, whipped cream, a long white feather and massage oil. A trail of pink and red rose petals led from the front door, up the stairs to what was presumably the bedroom.

The bedroom. Because there obviously wasn't one on this level. Noelle gulped. *Oh, Lord...*

"Umm, Judd?"

Having spied the Honeymooner's Special as well,

his face had gone comically blank. "What the hell?" he muttered.

"Are you sure we're in the right cabin?"

He walked over to the bar and peered at a note attached. "I didn't make the reservations," he said, shooting her a grim look. "But considering the key opened the door and this—" he waggled the note at her "—is addressed to Mr. and Mrs. Anderson, this is definitely the right cabin. I'm going to have to kill someone," he muttered under his breath, his expression blackening with every passing second. "Slowly, painfully throttle the life right out of them," he remarked through gritted teeth. A bark of laughter erupted from his throat, then he gave his head a disbelieving shake and looked heavenward, evidently for some divine intervention. "And to think I left the military to avoid doing just that."

Had she not been listening closely, she would have missed that last bit and, for whatever reason, she was certain it was significant. His face was a mask of irritation and outrage and there was a fleeting expression of sadness—a grimness around his especially beautiful mouth—that made her want to hug him, to offer some form of comfort.

His cell phone suddenly lit up on his waist, snagging his attention. "Yes, yes, I know, Jeb, I know.

Trust me, you're going to hear from me," he said, more to himself to her.

Noelle grinned at his exasperated expression. "Do you often talk to yourself? Or do you have an imaginary friend I can't see?"

His lips twitched. "Both." He blew out a heavy breath, then turned to look at her, his face a mask of forced cheerfulness. "Right," he said with a brisk nod. "I'm going to step outside and make a quick phone call."

She pitied the person on the other end of the line. She nodded. "Should I settle in or are we going to try to move?"

"I'm not sure," he said. "But we're definitely not going anywhere tonight. You take the bedroom," he told her. He gestured to the living room. "I'll take the couch."

Had she been less certain that she wouldn't need the distance, she would have argued with him—the couch was decent-sized, but would hardly be comfortable for a man as tall as he was—but self-preservation won out. She didn't need to be anywhere near his body and a bottle of massage oil. Her mind might actually crack and she'd ask him to let her rub him down and then slip and slide all over him.

"All right. Thanks," she added awkwardly, shoving a hand through her hair.

She felt his gaze skim over her face, lurk around her mouth. "Have you got everything you need out of the car?"

Lips still tingling from his lengthy perusal, she glanced at her bags next to the door. "I do."

He nodded once. "Then I'll see you in the morning. "

All righty then. Disappointment knifed through her. She should be relieved at the dismissal, Noelle thought. Should be happy that he didn't want her to hang around down here with him, that at least one of them appeared to have a little self-control. And he was definitely exercising it, which was admittedly rather gratifying. That raw look of desire she'd witnessed only hours ago combined with the hungry way he'd been staring at her mouth told her better than anything that she wasn't alone on this hellish island of lust.

He wanted her, too.

And they were here. In the Chalet of Love. Alone. With sex toys and chocolate and champagne.

She inwardly whimpered. She was going to need more than good intentions and self-control, Noelle thought. She was going to need a frontal lobotomy and a straitjacket.

Send For
2 FREE BOOKS
Today!

I accept your offer!

Please send me two free Harlequin® Blaze® novels and two mystery gifts (gifts worth about $10). I understand that these books are completely free—even the shipping and handling will be paid—and I am under no obligation to purchase anything, ever, as explained on the back of this card.

151/351 HDL FNN5

Please Print

FIRST NAME

LAST NAME

ADDRESS

APT.#   CITY

STATE/PROV.   ZIP/POSTAL CODE

Visit us online at
www.ReaderService.com

▼ If offer card is missing write to: The Reader Service, P.O. Box 1867, Buffalo, NY 14240-1867 or visit www.ReaderService.com ▼

NO POSTAGE
NECESSARY
IF MAILED
IN THE
UNITED STATES

BUSINESS REPLY MAIL
FIRST-CLASS MAIL   PERMIT NO. 717   BUFFALO, NY

POSTAGE WILL BE PAID BY ADDRESSEE

THE READER SERVICE
PO BOX 1867
BUFFALO NY 14240-9952

8

"WHAT'S WRONG?" his brother asked by way of greeting. "Has anything happened?"

Judd dropped heavily into one of the rocking chairs positioned on the front porch, ignoring the near freezing temperatures and watched his breath frost the air. "Depends on your definition of wrong," he said, his voice cracking with irritation.

Jeb paused, evidently considering both Judd's tone and his own response. "Why don't you give me your definition of wrong, little brother, and we'll go from there. I'm told the previous safe house went up in flames less than thirty minutes after you left."

"That's right. No doubt they got a hit on her GPS via her phone and picked up on it when she called Payne to ask to have me replaced." He laughed grimly. "I'm getting off to a *swimming* start, here," he said. "Just freaking fantastic."

"I heard about that," Jeb remarked, a smile in his voice. "I wouldn't worry about it. Payne's of the impression that Ms. Montgomery is headstrong and accustomed to doing things her own way."

He smiled, rubbed his eyes as he relaxed further into the chair. "Yeah, that's one way of putting it. I'd add sarcastic, stubborn, fiendishly clever and irritating as hell to the description." Naturally, he found all of those things wildly attractive. Who would have thought—have ever *dreamed*—that he'd be turned on by the sharp edge of her tongue, the mulish lift of her adorable chin, the wicked intelligence in those pale green eyes. Intelligence that, for the bulk of their brief acquaintance, had been spent trying to make him feel stupid.

Jeb hummed under his breath. "She's pretty, too, isn't she?"

Pretty? Judd blew out a breath, considered the ordinary adjective. It fit, certainly, but fell impossibly short of a true representation of who she was, how she looked. She wasn't just merely pretty—she was extraordinary. She was energy and light personified. Vitality in motion. Even when she was sitting perfectly still, there was a hum of...power, for lack of a better description, around her. His lips twisted. Almost radioactive.

He could *feel* it. Was inexplicably *drawn* to it.

He cleared his throat. "She's quite attractive. Long red hair, green eyes." Nice ass, beautiful breasts, a body a man could sink into without fear of getting jabbed by a protruding bone. He wanted to fall into her right now, dive dick first straight into her warm welcoming heat and stay there until he screamed hallelujah or his balls burst, whichever came first…so long as he did.

"And you want her," Jeb said, because there was no way he wouldn't know. If his brother could pick up on the smallest bit of frustration, then something as potent as the most singularly incredible sexual attraction he'd ever experienced was certainly fair game. After all, he'd known the minute Jeb met Sophie that his brother desperately wanted her.

Hell, *he'd* been awakened from a dead sleep with a hard-on. And he'd been alone at the time. *That* had never happened. And he'd never mentioned it to Jeb because it was just too damned…bizarre.

Because their twin connection had always been so strong, Judd was used to some pretty odd things. Like the time he'd had a sudden craving for a strawberry milkshake and Jeb had walked in with one in his hand, the straw stuck in his mouth. Or when Jeb had lost his retainer—had tossed it away with the remains of his school lunch for the second time— and he'd gotten so panicked while in his health class that he'd nearly hyperventilated during the Sex Ed video. Talk about mortifying. But the hard-on, for absolutely no reason, one obviously brought about by his twin's feelings?

That was new.

Had the same thing happened to Jeb? Judd wondered now. Had his reaction to Noelle been so substantial that Jeb had felt it as well? If so...then good enough for him, Judd thought, grinning. Better the both of them wonder instead of just him.

"She's hot," Judd finally admitted. "And infuriating and unpredictable."

His brother laughed. "In other words, she's not one of those biddable star struck yes-girls you usually end up taking to bed."

Judd scowled at the phone. "'Agreeable' is the word I think you're looking for."

"Mindless," Jeb countered, laughing softly. "Hell, that last girl I remember you hooking up with thought that those 'Slow—Children Ahead' signs in residential subdivisions referred to the *children*," he said incredulously, his voice cracking with humor. "*Not* the speed limit."

Yes, well, that was rather unfortunate, he'd admit.

Cherry certainly hadn't been the sharpest tool in the shed, but she'd made up for her dullness in other areas, if he remembered correctly.

And he usually did.

At any rate, that was neither here nor there. "Yeah, well, your taste hasn't always been as discerning as it is now," he told him. "Sophie is *miles* above par. Remember Sasha? The medium you brought to Thanksgiving dinner who told our grandmother that her aura was black?"

Jed guffawed. "That was priceless," he wheezed. "Gran was livid."

Yes, she had been. She'd imperiously ejected Sasha from the rest of the meal, then threatened to disinherit anyone else who so much as chuckled because they'd all been rolling in their seats, their parents included. Judd clearly remembered his mother leaning over and saying, "No doubt it matches her soul."

That was the trouble with some people and money—it made them bitter and crazy. Thank God, it hadn't affected their parents that way, Judd thought. Despite their undeniably impressive portfolios—and both he and Jeb had them as well—his parents had always lived well below their means and looked for happiness in other places. His grandmother, unfortunately, wielded her wealth like a club, her railroad pedigree like a better-than-you badge.

Money, on its own, could do nothing. It's how that money was spent that revealed its true power.

Noelle Montgomery, based on what he'd read of her activities and various donations, understood that better than a lot of people.

Was that the appeal? Beyond the beautiful body and impressively keen wit? Was it knowing that she was generous and willing to work hard? To go into ravaged areas and shift debris? Bandage cuts? Serve food? Offer a little of herself with every bit of human kindness?

"Is it just the sexual attraction or is there more there?" Jeb suddenly asked, seemingly tuning in to his thoughts once again. "Because if it's just sex, then you'd be better off looking for a little recreational knob polishing once this assignment is over. If it's more than that…" He trailed off leadingly. "Then that's another thing altogether."

And he'd know, Judd thought, particularly considering recent circumstances. Was it more than good old-fashioned lust? he wondered. He was intrigued, certainly. More so than he'd ever been about anyone. And she definitely had a way of pulling a reaction out of him. No indifference or any approximation thereof. He either wanted her with every fiber of his being, enjoyed their conversation more than he had any other…or wanted to pick her up and shake her.

No middle ground. No happy medium.

It was full-throttle, all or nothing.

And it was terrifying. And, more significantly, he'd *just* met her. Good grief…

A few more days spent in her company and he'd undoubtedly need to be put away in a padded room devoid of sharp objects. Especially if he was going to have to keep his hands off of her. Which reminded him…

"Who booked this cabin?" he asked, darting a look through the window, glaring at the "Welcome, Honeymooners" sign, specifically. That thing was coming down tonight, Judd thought. Post haste. He'd be damned before he'd sleep under the bloody thing.

Jeb hesitated, mulling it over. "I imagine that would have fallen to Juan-Carlos. Why? Is it unsuitable?"

"More like awkward," he told him, his gaze moving to the tall white feather in the basket on the counter. He imagined sliding it down the fluted hollow of Noelle's naked spine, slipping it over the inside of her thighs. His stomach and jaw simultaneously clenched, and he struggled to banish the vision, to hold on to any semblance of control. "Evidently the owners of the cabin are laboring under the incorrect assumption that Noelle and I are honeymooning here. They hung a big-ass banner off the balcony and left us a bottle of champagne and a lover's basket, complete with whipped cream and massage oil."

"You're kidding," Jeb said, his voice breaking with barely suppressed humor. "That's, uh…interesting," he finally finished.

"It's *hell*," Judd growled. "There's a trail of rose petals leading to the friggin' bedroom," he said, trying not to shout. "Notice I said *the* bedroom. As in *one*. I'm going to be kipping on a glorified love seat while Sleeping Beauty rests comfortably up in her tower."

"I'm sure that different accommodations can be arranged," Jeb told him. "I'll talk to Payne in the morning."

"No, don't," Judd said, pinching the bridge of his nose. "I'll make do. I've slept in worse conditions and I don't want to be any more trouble than I've already been."

"You haven't been any trouble. Believe me, they're all used to this. A woman can throw a wrench into an assignment faster than anything else. Try not to worry about it and just do your job. Keep her safe."

"I have every intention of it," he told his brother, resolved more than ever to do just that.

The mere idea that there was someone out there who had fired a bullet at her twice and tried to burn her to death—*twice*—made him want to roar with rage and break things.

He'd been concerned before he'd actually met her—recognized the injustice and danger of it. But now? Now that he'd met her, looked into those lovely green eyes and saw the fear and anger and frustration roiling in them? The hint of vulnerability in the stubborn lift of her chin? The brave way she continued to push on and do the right thing for no other reason than it was just that—the *right* thing…

Now he didn't just want to keep her safe—he wanted to rip the offender limb from limb, he wanted to tear off every crooked arm of Tubby Winchester's crooked business. He wanted to make the man pay, make him hurt. And the time would come, Judd was sure. He would see to it. In the interim, it was his job to keep her safe and out of harm's way.

The question was…who was going to protect him? Most especially from himself? Because something told him that, despite multiple tours of duty on foreign ground, he was in a more dangerous position right now—at this very moment—than he'd ever been in his life.

And he'd never been more tempted to sleep with the enemy.

But he couldn't. He could *not,* Judd repeated to himself. Because if he was this spun up and confused about her now—if she could tie him up in knots in a mere evening—then something told him that taking her to bed, finding the release and relief he most desperately wanted between her thighs, would result in a permanent, irrevocable snarl, one he grimly suspected he'd never be able to untangle.

And she'd be right in the heart of it.

"IF THAT bitch makes it to the courthouse alive, you're going to wish you were never born."

"I tried," Curtis snapped, drawing a concerned look from Lisa, his secretary. He got up, hurried around the desk and closed the door. With a paranoid glance over his shoulder, he retreated to the other side of the room and lowered his voice. His heart clamored in his chest, aching from the excess rush of adrenaline.

"It doesn't matter that you tried, Curtis. It only matters that you *failed*. There's a penalty for failure. Do you like pain, Curtis? Does pain turn you on?"

Oh, Jesus... "They'd left, damn you! They weren't there! If I'd had the information sooner I might have—"

The mystery caller tsked chillingly. "You aren't suggesting this is my fault, are you, Curtis? Because that would be a mistake. You dawdled, Curtis. You wasted ninety seconds after the call in your office, another hundred and eighty talking to those *delicious* little girls of yours—"

Curtis gasped in horror, certain he was going to be sick. Nausea clawed up the back of his throat.

"—then another thirty making nice with the wife. She could stand to lose a few pounds, but she's got great tits," the man on the line added silkily. "More than a mouthful. We've been making bets on those tits. I say her nipples are more brown than pink, but Patrick—the one who likes the knives, I think I've mentioned him before—he's convinced that they're the same color as her lips, a soft dusky rose. Who's right, Curtis? Me or Patrick? Never mind," he said dismissively. "I'm sure we'll find out."

He was shaking so hard he nearly dropped the phone. "You stay the hell away from my family, or I swear to God, I'll—"

"You'll what, Curtis? Kill me?" He laughed. "Because you've proven you're so good at that."

"I'll—"

"—go to the police?" he finished. "Go ahead," he taunted. "I dare you. You'll be dead before you get out of the parking lot and I'll personally see to it that your family is punished for your *stupid, reckless behavior*," he told him, his voice a low growl of anger. "The point is, Curtis, that you wasted five minutes in the house—*five* essential minutes—then another four when you went through the drive-thru to get your caramel macchiato at Peg's."

Curtis felt his rolling stomach drop to his knees and he collapsed once more into his chair. They were watching him? he thought wildly. Knew that he'd finished his cigarette, talked to his girls, chatted with his wife? Even went to get coffee? Oh, God… What had he gotten himself into? What had he done? How could he have been so unforgivably *stupid?*

This was Tubby Winchester, he reminded himself. Of course, they were watching him. Of course, they were.

"So here's the thing, Curtis," he went on in that same unnerving tone of voice. "We're beginning to wonder if your heart is really into taking care of this for us. We're beginning to wonder if you're taking this situation as seriously as you should."

He tried to swallow, sweat leaking from every pore. "I am," he said hoarsely. "I won't screw up again," he promised. "I-I'll take care of it."

He winced over the line. "That's what you said last time, so you can see how we'd find it difficult to believe you, right, Curtis? Do you understand our dilemma?"

"I understand," he said. "I do, really."

"All the same, we've decided an insurance policy is in order. Pick one of your girls, Curtis—doesn't matter which one—and hand her over. We'll give her back when the job is done."

"What? No! I—" He blanched, his vision blackening around the edges.

"Head between your knees, Curtis," he said, laughing softly as though he found this all vastly entertaining. "We wouldn't want you to pass out."

Alarmed, he glanced up, looked out the glass door of his office and scanned the area for the person on the other end of the line. Several people were chatting on cell phones, at the desk phones, all of them looking perfectly ordinary. Looking as though they hadn't just asked him to hand over one of his children or his wife.

"I won't do it," he said, anger bursting through him. "I said I'd take care of Noelle and I will. But I will not willingly give you a member of my family. I'd kill myself first."

"Tsk, tsk. Belated nobility doesn't become you, Curtis. But have it your way. I'll let Patrick pick one."

His eyes widened. "What?"

The line went dead.

He went numb with horror. Deadened with fear.

Two seconds later his phone rang again and he answered it without checking the display first. "Don't you dare touch my family, you hear me!" he shouted frantically. "Stay the hell away from—"

"Curtis?" his wife interrupted tentatively.

He blinked, straightened. "Carla? Is that you, honey?" His eyes stung, his breath came in heaving gasps.

"Yes," she said, seemingly cautious with concern. "Who did you think it was? What did you mean, don't touch your family?"

He cleared his throat. Swallowed around the lump lodged there. "A crank call," he said dismissively. "Just some idiot trying to rattle my cage. Probably someone I didn't approve for a loan. You know how these people can be," he added. What was one more lie?

"Yes, I do, but if someone is calling your cell phone and threatening your family, then you need to report it, Curtis. You need to file a complaint. Get it on record."

"I will," he lied. He wouldn't, because it wouldn't do any good. No one could protect them. They'd never be safe again and it was all his fault. *His sweet girls, his dear wife...* Their names—their fates, even—leaving the lips of mad men, of sociopaths, of perverts.

He tossed the phone down and retched.

"Curtis?" his wife's disembodied voice said from the phone. "Curtis, are you all right?"

No, and neither were they—they just didn't know it.

He wiped his mouth on his sleeve and picked up the phone once more. "Sorry," he said. "I think I'm coming down with something."

She made a sound of regret. "That's too bad. Mom called and wanted us to come to dinner tonight. She's bought the girls something for Christmas and wants to let them have it early, says she can't wait another week."

"They'll be thrilled." It felt odd to talk about something as ordinary as Christmas. Surreal, even. When had this happened? When had the ordinary stopped being ordinary?

"Dad won't be there," she continued. "He's got a meeting in Jackson tonight with some old Peace Corps buddies. I know it's a lot of estrogen to your testosterone, but it would be nice if you could go. You've been so busy lately."

Yes, busy trying to kill Noelle Montgomery. Whom his father-in-law had put firmly out of reach. If only he knew who the old man had hired to protect her, Curtis thought. If only he—

A thought struck. Ed gone, his office free, his computer with access to his email right there... And if that didn't reveal anything, then his internet history might, provided he hadn't cleared the cache recently. Hope bloomed.

Maybe all wasn't lost after all.

"I'd love to come with you," he said. "I've missed you and the girls. Have I told you that recently?" he asked her. "Have I mentioned that I love you, Carla?"

A little stutter of happiness echoed in his ear. "Not recently," she said. "I know it, of course, but it's nice to hear."

"I'm going to come home right now and do more than tell you, baby," he said. "I'm going to *show* you."

"*Curtis.*" Another titter of laughter. "Goodness, what's gotten into you?"

"Nothing," he lied. "It's just been too long since I've gotten into you. Put that red nightie on, the one with all the lace. I'll be there in five minutes."

"I—"

"And unplug the phone and close the blinds, would you? No distractions." Or onlookers.

It was time for Curtis to rediscover what color his wife's nipples were—gallingly, he couldn't remember—and the rest of the world could just fuck off for a while.

Most especially Tubby Winchester.

9

THOUGH SHE WOULDN'T have imagined it possible in such a small space with very limited choices available for entertainment, somehow Judd had managed to avoid her for the past two days. Oh, they'd shared meals, of course, but only because they both were conditioned to eating around the same time. And really, had he refused to put his feet under the table when she did, it would have been only too obvious that he was deliberately trying to stay away from her.

She knew why, of course. Saw it every time he looked at her, every time that black as sin gaze collided with hers or slipped scorchingly over her body.

Nevertheless, irrationally, his strictly professional behavior had hurt her feelings.

Which was ridiculous, she knew, but she couldn't seem to help herself. The portion of her brain responsible for logical thought was aware that his pulling back was more than likely a blessing in disguise— even if it didn't feel like one-and that she should congratulate herself on having a bodyguard who could hold fast to his resolve. She knew all of that, even secretly applauded his self-control because, admittedly, it was far more powerful than hers.

So why, then, had she been deliberately trying to sabotage him? To push him so far past the breaking point that he ultimately snapped? Why was she so hell-bent and determined to bend that iron will?

Because it *infuriated* her, Noelle ultimately concluded. She'd never cared about being irresistible before, but now suddenly—because of him—she did. She knew that everything about this impossible situation had gotten all twisted up in her head, knew she wasn't thinking rationally. She *knew*. And yet...

She *wanted*.

And, more importantly, she wanted him to want her so much that he jumped the chain and wanted her more.

The morning following their arrival, she'd awoken to no evidence of the honeymoon theme at all, other than the rose petals that had been left from inside her door to her bed. The ones leading up to it had been painstakingly picked up—it must have taken him hours to do it without the aid of a vacuum cleaner and, though she was a deep sleeper, she was relatively certain she would have heard that.

The banner had been taken down from the balcony railing, the basket and champagne gone from the bar. She would have liked to have had a little of that chocolate, Noelle thought, mildly perturbed, but she didn't dare ask about it because to do so would acknowledge that she'd noticed he'd made the changes. She was particularly concerned about the whereabouts of that feather—she'd spent entirely too much time picturing it against his skin—and hoped that he hadn't thrown it away. Ultimately, though, since he'd decided to pretend as if they weren't attracted to one another, pride prevented her from bringing it up.

But it didn't prevent her from going downstairs in her towel.

Often, with varying amounts of water on her skin.

She couldn't believe she was behaving so shamefully, but then she'd never met anyone like him before either. Anyone who tripped every single trigger, who made her thighs go weak with a single half-quirk of his lips—not even a full smile.

She'd probably collapse if he ever aimed one of those at her.

Of course, if he'd fall down on top of her, then it would be worth it.

Whistling tunelessly she padded through the living room, where he sat reading a book, and made her way into the kitchen to get a snack. Thankfully, Bud and Lucinda—the thoughtful owners of the chalet—had stocked several goodies for them. She was especially fond of the cheese straws.

She knew the exact moment when his gaze landed on her, could feel the prickly tightening of her skin, the quiver low in her belly. She swallowed as need welled up inside of her, filled her from the tips of her toes to the top of her head. Her breasts pebbled behind the fabric, went heavy with want and her mouth practically ached it was so desperate for the taste of his skin. She squeezed her eyes tightly shut, summoning patience from a nearly tapped-out well, then pinned a smile on her face and turned to look at him.

"Can I get you anything while I'm in here?" she asked, gesturing to the fridge.

His face was a stone cold mask free of expression, almost as if he'd willed it into paralysis.

His eyes, on the other hand, were not.

Mercy... They were darker even than usual—which she would have imagined would be impossible had she not been paying such close attention to them—and they burned with torment, blistered with hellish, feverish need.

"No, thank you," he said, the words clipped in

a low growl. He arched a brow, his smile knowing. "Taking another bath, are you?"

She lifted one shoulder in a lazy shrug, purposely allowing the towel to droop a little. "What can I say? I'm fond of that heart-shaped tub. It's roomy and the jets are nice."

His nostrils flared marginally. "Perhaps I should give it a try."

Her imagination obligingly called up that image. *Him. Hot, naked, wet, his massive muscular shoulders glimmering in candlelight... Dark hair slicked back off his hauntingly beautiful masculine face.*

She blinked, swayed a little, trying to draw him back into focus. "You should."

"Are you all right?" he asked innocently. "You look a little flushed."

"Other than being bored to tears, I'm fine," she told him, struggling to find her train of thought. It hadn't just derailed, it had vanished altogether. "I've read all the books your coworkers' wives sent, worked every crossword puzzle in the book and, though I've seen most of the movies, I suppose I'll go ahead and start on them."

"They added some clothes into that bag as well," he told her, glancing significantly at her towel. "You know," he said, "in case you wanted to put some on."

She bit her lip to hide her smile. "I found them,

thanks. That was very thoughtful. Please pass along my thanks until I can give them in person."

She *had* appreciated the care package. Because she'd literally left her house with only the clothes on her back, she'd had very little to wear over the past couple of weeks and what she'd been wearing had been picked up by Les, who'd been pretending to shop for his wife. Evidently Les's wife had been fond of floral patterns and since he'd not been certain of her size—even though she'd told him—he'd decided to err on the side of caution and the bulk of what he'd picked up for her was One Size Fits All. As a result, Noelle had dubbed her new wardrobe "Shower Curtain Chic."

The Ranger Security wives had done a much better job. They'd packed comfortable jeans and sweaters, pretty bras and panties, warm pajamas and a variety of high-end toiletries. They'd also included a sexy gown and a little box of condoms, along with a little note that said, "Just in case…"

Smart women, Noelle had concluded. But considering she was on birth control and Judd Anderson seemed to find her annoyingly resistible, they were a thoughtful but moot point. Did he know they'd put the condoms in there? Noelle wondered. Along with the cotton swabs, first aid kit and manicure set? Somehow she doubted it. The thought made her grin.

"I'll be sure to let them know. Does everything fit?" he asked, referencing the clothes once more, seemingly determined to make his point.

"Everything fits," she said. And that was all.

A muscle jumped in his jaw. "Right. Excellent."

"I don't suppose we could go for a walk later, could we? Just to get out of here for a little while?" She was going stir crazy, needed to breathe some un-recycled air.

His gaze had dropped to her legs, seemed particularly drawn to the skin just above her knee. "Perhaps," he said, his voice gratifyingly unsteady. "You're not planning on wearing the towel, are you?"

Noelle grinned, bit the inside of her cheek. "Probably not. Too chilly. Much like the atmosphere around here recently," she remarked pointedly. She knew what he was doing and she knew why. Better that he should know that, she decided. She jerked her chin toward the bedroom. "I'll go back upstairs," she said with a dramatic little wince. "Try to stay out of your way."

He shifted uncomfortably. "You're not in my way," he said, but he didn't meet her gaze and they both knew it wasn't true.

"Liar," she said with good humor. "That's all right, though. I enjoy my own company." And she did— she'd had to learn how, especially without siblings and having parents who were more confused by her than anything else—but she'd be the liar if she said she didn't want to spend time with him. If she said she didn't want him with every cell in her body. If she said that the attraction was purely a physical one, because she had sense enough to know that wasn't true. Did she want him?

God, yes.

But it was more than that and she knew it. There was something about him that called to her on more than a physical level, an elusive "it" factor that made her want to know him better. That same little inexplicable nugget of insight told her he was a man worth knowing, that given the chance, he could be more than a potential bed mate, more than a fleeting friend.

He could be special.

To complicate matters, she was still rabidly curious about what made him tick, what had made him leave the military. She still hadn't forgotten the little cryptic comment he'd made the first night of their arrival. Something to the effect of he was going to have to kill someone and he'd changed careers to avoid doing just that.

Had that been it, truly? Noelle wondered. Had he lost his stomach for war? The death and destruction? Because, while she appreciated every last man and woman who was currently serving or had ever served, she damned sure didn't envy them their job. There was comfort, she was sure, in knowing that one was nobly serving one's country, contributing to a greater good.

But walking into the line of fire, aiming one's own weapon and taking a life, not to mention the long months away from loved ones…

Eek. Give her a good old natural disaster any day.

She looked at him once more, tracing the lines of his unbelievably handsome face, appreciating the contrast between his flawless skin and dark, sleek hair. He was almost too beautiful to look at, Noelle thought. Too…*everything* to be real and not just a figment of her imagination. An odd ache suddenly tightened in her chest and she sucked in a tiny breath, alarmed at the emotion tensing there.

"I enjoy it," he said, a question forming in his eyes as she continued to stare at him.

She blinked. "Sorry, what?"

"Your company," he said. His gaze tangled significantly with hers, dropped to her lips and then bounced up once more. "Too much," he admitted, with an endearingly rueful smile, one that shared that adorable dimple. "Which is the problem."

Well, at least he'd admitted it, Noelle thought, marginally mollified. She'd known, of course, but having him confess it made her all the more aware of him, all the more aware of…everything. Recent events, for obvious reasons, had forced her to look at life differently, with a more temporal eye. She was now more afraid of missed opportunities than making mistakes, of saying no when she should say yes, of standing still instead of leaping into the fray.

This was a Leap Moment.

Had she met him prior to the multiple attempts on her life, Noelle knew she wouldn't have been so bold. She would have been more cautious, weighing every possible outcome to every possible scenario. She would have wanted him, sure—the attraction was simply too potent to deny—but *acting* on that attraction? Rolling the dice? Who knew?

But she knew now. And she'd been adding more and more things to her newly formed Life's Too Short List.

Most recently, *him*.

Whether she came out of this alive, whether she ever saw him again beyond the trial, she knew beyond a shadow of a doubt that she'd never—*never*—feel this sort of desire again. This mindless, desperate, achy bone-melting need was a direct result of *him*. *He* was the key.

And oh, how she wanted to pull him into her lock.

Her lips curved with perceptive humor and she

shrugged negligently again, then started toward the stairs. "Pity," she said. "It's not for me."

SHE WAS TOO damned clever by half, Judd thought, watching Noelle saunter up the stairs, her delicious bare-beneath-the-towel rump swaying fetchingly with every step.

Of course, it wouldn't be a problem for her, he thought, resisting the urge to tear his hair out. What did she have to lose, ultimately?

Nothing. Nada. *Zilch.*

Whereas, he, on the other hand could potentially lose… He frowned, his mouth watering as she sent him another almost pitying smile. *You poor, ignorant fool,* it taunted. His brow furrowed in confusion. What was it again he stood to lose? He was certain he'd had good reasons for avoiding her for the past two days.

He must have, otherwise he'd been torturing himself for nothing. Putting himself through this self-sentenced hell for nothing. Denying himself for nothing. So why had he done it? It couldn't have been his job, because each and every one of the Ranger Security men had found their significant others on an assignment for the company.

Not a single one of them—his brother, in particular—could cast a stone.

Self-preservation, maybe? He felt his expression fall. Oh, yeah. Definitely self-preservation, he decided remembering their first encounter and the subsequent car ride here. The off-the-charts sexual attraction, the way his balls had drawn up and his dick had instantly moved into the launch position the instant he'd seen her, not to mention the whole planets-colliding-in-space-thing when she'd looked at him. His new intergalactic princess. His new gravity, because heaven knew he was uncontrollably drawn to her. Drawn to her light, drawn to her energy, drawn to her goodness. He'd spied the tattoo on the inside of her right wrist last night over dinner—which she hadn't eaten in her towel, thank God—and the message she'd chosen to put there haunted him. It was a tree, very well drawn and well defined, the word "Hope" written in the carefully arranged branches.

He'd wanted to ask her if it was a reminder to always have hope, or to share it with others. Had there been any particular inspiration or had she simply had a little too much to drink and drunk-inked. Somehow he doubted it. Hope, he thought again. Was there hope for him, really? he wondered. Because after losing his nerve at the trigger, after tallying all those kill shots for God and country, he had to wonder.

She, he knew, didn't have to wonder. She was the angel *in* the darkness, not the Angel of Death. Add in that kind, unfailing, hardworking and generous nature along with that fiendishly clever little mind and World's Best Ass and she was the total package.

Hell, he'd known the first instant he'd clapped eyes on her that she was different—an "other" who defied a category—and, better still, that he was in trouble. He'd just been too damned arrogant to admit it.

But protecting his own sanity from certain corruption was smart, right? And denying himself, when she clearly wanted him as much as he wanted her, was noble, wasn't it? Self-sacrificing, even. He gritted his teeth.

Particularly when she'd been parading around the place in a damned towel and little else for the past couple of days, her fiery hair pulled into a messy ball on top of her head, revealing the sleek column of her throat, the silky skin beneath her jaw.

He'd mentally taken her in every room in this cabin, in every possible sexually depraved position— some of which he was fairly certain weren't even physically possible. Had even imagined bending her fine ass over the front porch rail, plunging into her from behind while enjoying the majestic mountain view, the scent of crisp air and freshly brewed coffee in the breeze.

Impossibly, he hardened further. Need ballooned inside of him, filling him from the inside out, spreading like wildfire through his perpetually feverish blood. She was up there now, Judd thought. Probably naked. In that confounded heart-shaped tub built for two.

A sex tub.

So, what exactly, was he doing down here again? He blinked, swallowed thickly. Wavered. Oh, to hell with it, he thought, tossing his book aside and vaulting off the couch. She didn't want him avoiding her? Fine. He'd do the opposite, by God.

He'd friggin' *invade* her.

10

NOELLE HEARD THE smack of something hit the floor, then the sound of quick footfalls on the steps and a little thrill whipped through her middle. Other than to shower—which he did right after she got out of bed first thing in the morning—he hadn't been upstairs at all.

It was almost as though he'd deemed it enemy territory.

But he was coming now, she thought. And he was coming fast. The door swung open and he suddenly filled the frame, his gaze meeting hers in the vanity mirror. It was hot and heavy lidded, but more significantly, determined.

She arched a brow. "Change your mind about the tub?"

"Later," he said, sidling toward her in a loose-hipped swagger that suggested his dick was too big to dangle between his thighs, stripping his shirt off over his head and tossing it aside like it didn't matter. She gulped.

It didn't. Good Lord...

Beautiful skin and well-honed muscle all wrapped perfectly around the most incredible bone structure she'd ever beheld. Some sort of tribal tattoo she was determined to inspect closer encircled his left biceps and dark hair barely dusted his pecks, then met in the middle of his chest and bisected his abs in a faint line that disappeared below his waistline. His hand immediately dropped to the snap at his jeans, easily flicking the button open as he made his way to her.

His gaze never left hers.

Her stomach flipped over as need washed through her, tumbling her insides like ocean waves. She turned around, leaned against the vanity counter and lifted her chin, a smile twitching over her lips as anticipation rose. "Deciding to embrace my clothing optional approach to protective custody?" she asked.

He crowded her, getting so close that she could smell him, feel the heat coming off of his skin. But didn't touch her.

It was agony.

His gaze slid over her face, lingered around her jaw, her mouth, then found her eyes once more. His were intense, brooding and, oddly enough, a little guarded. "I'm only going to ask this once, so consider your response before letting it leave your lips."

She nodded.

"Is this really what you want?"

She would have thought that would have been obvious, but did as he asked and checked the thought before she said it. Because he wasn't asking if she wanted him—that went without saying—he was asking if she wanted what would come after. The change in the status quo, because intimacy—even that of the fleeting variety—changed things. Sometimes for better, sometimes for worse. But the act of sharing one's body, however freely given, was never without some sort of consequences, some sort of expectation. Noelle released a shaky breath, ignored the tiny voice of warning in her head, the one telling her that she'd never be the same after being with him.

She knew that.

But she'd risk it.

"I do," she said.

He smiled then—really, truly smiled—making her heart stumble in her chest, then uttered a growl of pleasure, and picked her up and set her on top of the vanity counter. She loved that he could do that so easily. It thrilled her, that blatant masculine show of strength. She reached out, slid a shaky hand over his chest, felt pleasure boil up within her.

"I'm clean and protected," she said, her gaze feasting on him. "You?"

"Passed my last physical with flying colors," he told her, lifting her chin with a single touch of his finger. Sensation sizzled through her. His hungry gaze clung to her mouth, darkened with desire, then he cupped her face, his skillful fingers pushing into her hair as he lowered his mouth a mere millimeter away from hers.

He hesitated, not out of indecision, she knew, but something else. And she knew what that something else was—knew that it was as equally nameless as it was significant.

Then his lips touched hers and all thought fractured and fled.

Though she knew it was impossible, the world seemed to shake around her—shift—but *she* didn't move, she held firm, safe and protected, on what felt like the only solid ground she'd ever known.

Wonder and awe tangled with need and desire and she wrapped her arms around him, pulling him closer to her. Another little masculine growl sounded between their joined lips and he stroked her face as he fed at her mouth, slid his fingers along the sensitive underside of her neck. She detected the smallest, *bar-*

est tremble in his big hands, his long fingers, and something about that betraying vibration burrowed into her heart, making it swell with emotion.

He didn't just kiss—he made love to her mouth. He'd mastered the art of suckling and sliding his lips over hers, wrapping his tongue around hers with that ever elusive exact moisture-to-lips ratio. It was the perfect balance—not too wet, not too dry—but the sweet spot in between.

And, oh, how sweet it was…

She deepened the kiss, tracing his face with her hands, thumbing the soft hollow just below his cheek bone, the sleek skin above his brow. Moisture slickened her folds and a quivering warmth stole into her sex and settled there, leaving an achy weight in her womb, a desperate sense of anticipation. She felt the long length of him nudge against her through his jeans. She widened her legs and reached between them, cupping him.

He sucked in a breath, growled as she lowered his zipper. His jeans sagged on his lean hips and he jutted forward, extra hard, extra long and extra thick.

Proportionate, she thought, drunk with desire. Drunk on him.

She took him in hand, worked the slippery skin against her palm and he flexed forward, giving her more. He left off her mouth, raining open-mouthed kisses along her jaw and down her neck, then tugged the towel open, revealing her naked body to his greedy gaze.

Impossibly, his black eyes darkened even more, his supremely carnal mouth curled in hungry appreciation, and she felt the change in him instantly, felt the urgency as he figuratively switched gears. He'd been idling, savoring, a foot over the brake, as it were, to appreciate her, this.

Them.

But he'd just moved into overdrive.

The banked hum of power was there in his touch, the blind need for speed, the ultimate race for release.

She scooted forward, opening herself up to him even more as his hot mouth found her breast. His lips closed over her, tugging at the puckered bud, sending a spasm of sensation directly to her core. She gasped, pulled him closer, sliding her hands over his skin, measuring muscle and bone. He reached between them, slipped a finger over her weeping folds, her engorged clit, tormenting her with pleasure.

She closed her eyes against the onslaught of sensation, felt his tongue slide down her belly, then knocked her toiletries to the floor and cried out as his mouth fastened over her sex. He opened her up to him, hooking her legs over his shoulders, which was just as well because she didn't have any strength left in them, and held her body rigid as he flicked his clever tongue over her clit, flayed it roughly, then suckled. She jerked, inhaled sharply as bliss knifed through her.

Just when she thought she couldn't possibly take anymore, when the pleasure was so debilitating it bordered on pain, he slipped a finger deep inside of her and moaned against her. "So wet," he breathed brokenly. "And you taste *so* damned good."

He felt so damned good. She whimpered, desperate for more. Desperate for him.

"Judd," she gasped. "Please. I need—" He hooked his finger around, pressed deeper and stroked some hidden part of her, a place so sensitive she was certain she'd never encountered it before. She could feel her feminine muscles contracting around him, could feel the beginning of climax quicken deep in her womb.

"Oh, *dammit*," she groaned, pounding her fist against the vanity as he continued his hedonistic assault. "*Son of a*—" Her breathing came in short, fast gasps, her body trembling on the brink of release. She was almost there, Noelle thought, gritting her teeth. Oh, Jesus. She wasn't— She couldn't— She wiggled, squirmed, her whole body on fire with need.

Just when she was a single stroke away of his wicked finger, he withdrew and stood. The protest died on her lips as he grasped her hips, hauled her forward and plunged into her, sliding hard and deep.

She nearly fainted.

Her breath seized in her lungs and every cell in her body sang with joy, with happiness, with an odd sort of homecoming, as though it had been waiting for this moment—this extraordinary recognition—her entire life and she hadn't known it until right now.

She looked up at him, caught his fierce, startled expression. Desperation, awe, need and wonder. She saw it all, understood his confusion because she was just as shocked, just as jolted by the singularly unique joining of their bodies.

His jaw locked, his hips flexed rhythmically, fast furious strokes that rattled the cabinets below the vanity. She absorbed them greedily, clamping her muscles around him with every indomitable thrust. It was wild and mindless, gritty and a little dirty, unlike anything she'd ever experienced before. She was more aware of her own body, her own pleasure while being fully plugged in to his as well.

Intimate, she decided. Because of the rawness, the stripped-down need? Or in spite of it? Either way, she didn't care. She just knew she'd never felt more connected to anyone else before. Knew that she'd never have sex again or take another partner without comparing it to this—to what she felt with him.

She'd no sooner formed the thought when she came, the orgasm erupting through her, waves of heat boiling like lava through every locked-down muscle in her body. Her mouth opened in a scream, a growl so low and elemental she barely recognized it coming from her own lips.

She fisted around him, hanging on for dear life, knowing that from this instant onward it—the life she'd painstakingly crafted and protected—would never, ever be the same.

JUDD FELT HER incredibly sweet, incredibly responsive body tighten around his, watched her expression as the climax ravaged her. Tension and release vibrated off her lush frame, squeezed him with her satiny heat. Her long wet hair hung in a tangled curtain down her back, her heart-shaped rear and small waist visible to him from the mirror.

He'd never seen anything so sexy, so hot, so beautiful in his life.

She. Was. Glorious.

Uninhibited, unrestrained, unreserved. She reveled in her womanliness, celebrated her sexuality, wasn't afraid to let him see how he made her feel. Hell, wasn't afraid to *feel*. To rise on the tide and let it take her where it wanted to go.

She was unequivocally, hands down, bar none *the* best lover he'd ever had. And they were only getting started.

Admittedly, he'd known that she was going to be different—after all, she'd been different from the start, hadn't she? He'd known that any woman who was capable of making him feel so much—from one end of the spectrum to the other—wasn't going to be an unremarkable lay.

He'd *known,* which was no small part of the reason he'd hesitated and tried to stay away from her.

But knowing something and being prepared were two completely different animals and nothing this side of heaven—or hell for that matter—could have prepared him for the molecular reconfiguration of his entire body merely kissing her had wrought.

Just kissing her.

In that nanosecond before his lips had touched hers, he'd felt the beginning of the impending change. The energy had shifted in the air around them, the hair on the back of his neck had prickled, then drawn in—unable to help himself—Judd had closed the distance between them and…that was it.

He'd come undone.

Her hands were soft and sure, her body a playground of sexual delight and the look in those pale green eyes when he'd finally—blessedly—pushed into her was something he'd never forget. He'd plunged into her tight, wet heat, felt her clamp around him, almost as though her body somehow recognized his, an innate familiarity that had swept through him like a plume of smoke on the tail end of a comet.

Shaken didn't begin to cover it.

His world had shifted again, the walls tilting around him, but it was warm and wonderful between her thighs and he'd held firm, his hands on her luscious hips, while he waited for everything else to settle.

She'd tightened around him over and over, urging him on with her soft cries of pleasure, her base growls of gratification. She swore, she begged, she hummed like a damned tuning fork and it was because of *him*.

Because she wanted him.

Because she was so into him she didn't care if her girly products hit the floor, she didn't care that she was on a friggin' sink instead of a soft bed, she didn't care that he'd dropped between her legs and ate her from the damned counter.

She only cared about what he did to her, what he was going to do next, how he made her feel.

He pounded into her again and again, the back of his balls so tight he feared they were going to burst. He glanced down at their joined bodies, her milky white thighs around his waist, that thatch of bright red curls framing his cock as he pushed into her glistening pink flesh.

He locked his jaw so hard he could have sworn he heard it crack.

Her gorgeous breasts bounced on her chest with each furious push into her body and her nipples matched her mouth, both a puckered raspberry pink. He loved the way they looked, perched on top of the creamy globes of her breasts like a cherry on top of a sundae.

She beat the counter with her fist, thrashed beneath him, squeezed him until she screamed. She tightened, every muscle seemingly frozen in shock, in awe of sensation, then she smiled and swore again, going boneless. She looked sated, relieved. Beautiful.

And that's what did it for him.

Judd came hard, the orgasm firing from his loins like an arrow released from a compound bow. He angled deep, pressed hard, locking himself inside her so far it was a miracle he was going to be able to extricate himself without some sort of surgical help.

His vision blackened around the edges but she glowed, his angel—she *glowed*. His knees, which had never failed him before, went weak. His thighs shook and his scalp tingled.

He didn't just feel the orgasm in his dick—he felt it all over.

Profoundly.

Judd roared in satisfaction, the sound almost inhuman and guttural, then wrapped her up and held her close while the storm whirled around them. He was holding the epicenter, he thought, a weak smile tugging at his lips. She clung to him, kissed his chest, his shoulder, a smile on her wicked lips. He reluctantly withdrew, picked her up and carried her to the bed, then laid her down and took the spot beside her.

She grinned, released a pent-up breath. "There," she said, as though she'd been a patient teacher and, he, a reluctant pupil. "Don't you feel better?"

He laughed, rolled onto his back and brought her with him, tucking her firmly against his chest. "Unquestionably," he told her. "What about you? Are you through walking around in your towel now?" he drawled.

"Yes." She doodled her fingers over his chest and sighed. "From now on I'm just going to walk around naked."

He felt his eyes widen, another chuckle working its way up his throat. He shrugged, contented. "Works for me."

In fact, *she* worked for him. On every level. And work had never felt so good.

11

CURTIS LOOKED AT the image on his cell phone and felt chubby swell in his pants. They were cotton candy pink, he thought, staring at a picture of his wife's breasts, her nipples. He still couldn't believe that she'd let him take the photos—that she'd trusted him enough with something so personal—and yet she did.

He didn't deserve her trust, though. Not really. Granted he'd never cheated on her—and could honestly say that he'd never been tempted—but there were other ways to cheat. Other ways to break promises and be false. He'd done that and more. He'd lied about what he'd been doing, where he'd been going, the excess money in the bank—fabricated bonuses that had never happened. He'd broken the law for Tubby Winchester, despite putting on the facade of being a decent man.

And he'd tried to kill Noelle Montgomery four times. And the hell of it? The sad part in all of this?

There was no easy way out, unless he wanted to kill himself. Then who would protect his family? Who would keep Patrick-who-liked-to-play-with-knives from his wife and daughters? No, the only way out was to do what he'd said he'd do—kill Noelle.

While he hadn't had the opportunity to break into his father-in-law's office the night before last—Carla had been particularly affectionate after their wonderful afternoon together and had kept him close to her side the entire night—thankfully, he was going to get another crack at it this evening. He was certain that Ed's computer—his email, in all likelihood—would produce the information Curtis needed. The key to finding Noelle—who seemed to have simply vanished into thin air—was finding out who his father-in-law had hired to protect her. From there, he was confident that he could get what he needed, the information that would lead him to her.

Curtis had suggested to his wife that she should invite her folks over to dinner at their house, to repay them for the lovely meal. It had been too long, he'd said. It would be wonderful to sit down to a meal she'd cooked, to have the kids and her parents all gathered round their table.

Which was all true—he rather liked his in-laws—

but it wasn't the reason he'd wanted her to invite them. He'd wanted her to invite them over because that would leave their own house empty. He'd be able to claim he was running late, then sneak into their house and into Ed's office.

His plan went off without a hitch. He waited at the end of the cul-de-sac and watched his in-laws leave, then quickly pulled into their driveway and around the back, hiding his car. He found the key in the usual hiding spot, let himself in, then quickly made his way into Ed's inner sanctum. The scent of money and good tobacco hung in the air and framed pictures of his family sat on the desk.

It hurt to look at his family, to know what his mistakes could potentially cost them.

He fired up the computer, plugged in a variety of passwords for the email program until he hit upon the right one—his wife's name—then started looking. He hit pay dirt a few clicks in.

Ranger Security. Atlanta-based. He whistled low, inspecting the quote. And damned expensive.

His cell phone rang, making him jump and his heart leapt into his throat. Hands shaking, he checked the display. *Carla*. He ignored the call, would return it from the car.

He scanned a few more emails, but nothing else from the security company was there. Either Ed had deleted them, or written correspondence had switched to strictly verbal. Probably the latter, he thought.

His phone rang again, echoing in the silence like a gunshot and he jumped once more. "Shit," he muttered, wiping a hand over his face. Not Carla this time. It was Tubby's mouthpiece.

He'd be sorry if he didn't answer this call and was too afraid to find out how much.

"Hello."

"What are you doing in your father-in-law's office?" the man asked. "You know, since he's at your house and that's where you're supposed to be. A cozy family dinner, I'm told. It pisses me off that I wasn't invited. Haven't I been good to you, Curtis? Don't you realize I'm the only thing standing between you and a toe tag?"

If this guy was the only thing keeping him alive, then he was in trouble, Curtis thought. Because the man was certifiable. Crazy as a shit house rat as his grandfather used to say.

"I needed to get a look at Ed's computer," he said. "It's been quite useful." It was nice not to sound like an incompetent fool, Curtis thought, pleased with his amateur sleuthing.

"Oh," he asked, his tone immediately changing. "How so?"

"I've found the company Ed hired to protect her," he told him. "Now it's merely a matter of finding out where they've put her."

"And you think that's going to be easy?"

"I think it's better than not knowing where to start," he snapped. "Let me handle it."

"What agency?" he asked. "We've checked all of our channels and came up empty-handed."

Curtis didn't know why, but he hesitated, not wanting to share his information. "I'll let you know if I run into a problem," he improvised. "In the interim, leave me alone. I'll contact you again when I have information."

"I'll contact you any time I want to," the man said, his voice going hard. "Your deadline has been moved up. The D.A. got the trial date moved to Friday."

Curtis blanched. "Friday? But how? Why?"

"Because of the multiple failed attempts on Noelle's life. 'Imminent danger to witnesses,' the D.A. argued. And won. You either kill her tomorrow or it's a sad funeral for you and your whole family. Wouldn't that be a shame, especially since you and your wife remembered you were married and started bumping uglies again. She's a tiger in the sack, isn't she?" he said. "I liked that face she made when you bent her over the bed. It was hot."

What the hell? There was no way he could have

seen them. The blinds had been closed, the curtains drawn. They'd been alone. How did—

Cameras, Curtis thought. No doubt his house and office had been outfitted and bugged when he'd gone to work for Tubby, to make sure that he kept his word and did as he was told. And as an information gathering tool, he imagined it worked well. It gave them leverage.

As if they needed more.

"Tomorrow is too soon. There's no way I can—"

"Find a way."

The line went dead.

Curtis hung his head and cried.

NOELLE BREATHED IN the mulchy sent of decaying leaves and cold air, huddled deeper into her jacket as they strolled along the creek they'd crossed via the bridge on the way in. Squirrels scrambled through the crunchy layer of fallen leaves, the sound especially loud in the resounding quiet. A couple of does stood on the rise above them, still as stones, unsure of whether to bolt or ignore them, while a pair of chipmunks argued on a fallen log.

Life, everywhere, despite the absence of summer.

"You were right," he said, his arm slung comfortably over her shoulder.

"Yes, I know."

He chuckled. "Do you even know what I'm talking about?"

"I don't have to." She smiled up at him. "I'm usually right, even when I'm wrong, or hadn't you noticed?"

"Oh, I've noticed," he said. "But in this instance I'm referring to suggesting we take a walk." He gave her a squeeze. "This is nice. It reminds me a bit of my sister-in-law's farm." He made a face. "Well, my brother's now, too."

"Oh?" She was hoping if she didn't ask a lot of probing questions he'd forget he was actually sharing a bit of personal information with her. These were the things she'd been dying to hear, the little bits of history that made him who he was, the man he'd become.

He kicked at a pine cone with a square-toed black boot, sent it skittering across the ground where it landed with a thud against a tree. Dressed in a pair of faded but comfortable jeans and a black fishbone cable knit sweater with one of those sexy shawl-type collars, he looked like he'd stepped off the cover of a men's fashion magazine.

She had no idea how much his clothes cost, but she recognized quality when she saw it. That, combined with the Tag Heuer watch encircling his wrist told her that he was in an income bracket well above most. Was it family money? she wondered. Not that he hadn't earned a comfortable living in the military—she was sure he did—but she didn't think the salary would accommodate such expensive tastes.

"Yes," he told her. "Sophie's offered me a bit of land out on their place, but…" He hesitated, his brow furrowing. "I don't know. They're newly married. I wouldn't want to get in the way."

"How big is her farm?"

"A couple hundred acres, I think."

Noelle choked on a laugh. "It sounds like they've got room. It's not like you'd be pulling a double wide trailer into their back yard."

He chuckled. "No, I suppose not."

He held a branch out of her way, then laced his fingers through hers. It was nice. Funnily enough, she'd had the devil's own time getting him to touch her, but now that he had, he couldn't seem to keep his hands off of her. She liked it. "You and your brother are close, right?"

His eyes widened significantly and he sent her a grin. "Too close for comfort sometimes," he said, somewhat cryptically. She knew he'd gotten a text from him a few minutes after they'd left the bedroom. Whatever the message had said, Judd's response had been a smiling, "Smug bastard."

"You'd mentioned you were twins," she remarked.

She squatted down and picked up a long branch, broke the end off to form a make-shift walking stick. "But not identical. Heaven and Hell, you'd said." She slid him a pointed look. "I would beg to differ on that score," she told him. "You're positively heavenly in a hellish sort of way."

He bit into his bottom lip. "Right."

"You are," she said. "You're beautiful. I'm sorry, but there's no better word for it," she told him when he shot her an incredulous look. "Not in a girly way, obviously," she continued. "In a virile, manly way."

He rolled his eyes. "Now you're patronizing me."

"I'm not! I'm just—" She shook her head, struggling to find the right words. "You're hard to describe," she finally told him. "The normal adjectives don't work. It's your bone structure, your coloring. And your eyes. They're strikingly black. My stomach gets all fluttery when you look at me," she confided. "And I don't flutter easily." She frowned. "In fact, I've never fluttered like that before."

There, she thought. He could read into that what he would.

He paused and turned to look at her, masculine pleasuring clinging to his lips. Lips she'd kissed, lips that had fed at her breasts and between her legs. A hot rush of sensation zipped into her core, making her thighs clench.

"Is that right?" he asked, his black as sin eyes glittering with satisfaction.

"Don't fish for more," she said, resuming their trek. "Accept the compliment and say thank you."

"That sounds like an order," he said, then tsked. "Double standard, eh?"

"It was advice," she said. "I don't give orders. I offer my opinions and make suggestions." It was bullshit and she knew it. So did he, evidently, because he chuckled and shook his head.

"You're a piece of work, you know that?"

"Thanks," she said pointedly. "See how that works? See how easy that is?"

He grinned and nodded at her. "Thank you. I love that I can make you shudder."

It was her turn to roll her eyes. "Flutter," she corrected. But shudder worked just as well, she supposed, chewing the inside of her cheek. He'd certainly done that, too. She'd fluttered and shuddered and quivered and quaked until she'd practically melted into goo. He'd pulled the best orgasm she'd ever experienced out of loins, made every particle in her being sing in sensation.

"Is there a difference?" he asked, his eyes twinkling with humor.

She nodded sagely, as though she knew something

he didn't. "Definitely. I'll have to show you some-time."

His smug little smile lost some of its edge. He swallowed. "You could show me now," he said, tug-ging her toward him.

Warmth slid through her. "We have on too many clothes."

He groaned, closed his eyes. "You're *evil*."

She went up on tippy toe and whispered hotly in his ear, "I prefer depraved." He shook, his eyes clos-ing, and he sucked a harsh breath in between his teeth.

"I think I just shuddered."

"Nope, that was a tremble. It's going to take my mouth on a more prominent organ to make you shud-der."

His eyes widened, then he chuckled darkly. "I'm standing by my 'evil,'" he said, giving his head a small shake. His gaze turned inward, probably imag-ining her mouth wrapped around his dick, then he shook himself. "Jesus. You're *killing* me."

"But I haven't done anything yet. Tell me about this farm," she said. "Are you going to build a house out there?"

She watched his mind switch gears, felt the pad of his thumb slide over the inside of her wrist. "I don't know. I haven't decided yet. I've got an apartment in

Atlanta. It's in the office building, so it's definitely convenient." He grimaced. "I'm not a big fan of the city, though. I'd rather have a little room to breathe. Get away from the noise."

She certainly understood that. "That's what I like about Mossy Ridge," she said. "It's relatively quiet. Even off the town square, where I live."

"Have you always lived in Mossy Ridge?"

She shot him a look. "You know the answer to that question. I'm sure it was in my file," she said drolly. The dreaded file. It reduced her life to a few pages. She hated the very idea of it.

"It was," he admitted, his gaze shrewd and assessing. "But it only listed the facts, not the way you felt about them."

Ah. Pleasure bloomed in her chest. So he wanted to know her better, too? It was insane how much that thrilled her. "True," she conceded. "Other than my tour with the Peace Corps immediately following high school, then my four years at Ole Miss, yes, I have always lived in Mossy Ridge." She cut him a glance. "But I didn't always want to. I was the typical teenager who firmly believed that the grass was always greener somewhere else—anywhere else— but home."

That bit had been true, as far as living with her parents was concerned. But once she'd moved back to town after she'd graduated and gotten her own place, she'd enjoyed being a part of the community when she wasn't in the field, when she wasn't volunteering somewhere.

He inclined his dark head knowingly. "I'd pegged you for a rebel."

Her lips curled. "I wasn't a rebel," she argued. "I was—"

"—a free spirit," he supplied.

"Tired of my parents," she finished. "Nothing so glamorous as a free spirit, I'm afraid."

His expression never wavered, but she felt his interest sharpen. "There was very little information on them in your file," he said.

There wouldn't be, she thought. Because they played so little role in her life. "I don't see them often," she said, careful to keep her tone casual. "We had different visions on how I needed to live my life. It wasn't that we just didn't see eye to eye—we weren't even looking at the same picture."

He was quiet for a moment. "What did they want you to do?"

"Get a job, stop volunteering and giving my money away."

He released a little breath, winced. "Stop being you, in other words."

Noelle stilled, turned to look at him. "Yes," she

breathed, astonished, her gaze searching his. Sweet God, he *got* it. He totally got it. He understood. She'd known him less than seventy-two hours and he'd only read the "facts" of her file…and he understood her better right now than her parents ever had. Had a better grasp of what was important to her, what made her tick more than anyone she'd ever met.

It thrilled her.

Unnerved her.

What else did he see? Noelle wondered. What other hidden truths had she unwittingly shared with him? What else had his keen mind noticed about her and stored away?

It was time to make the flow of information a little more equitable, she thought. Because, other than the fact that he had a twin brother and an apartment in downtown Atlanta, but preferred the country, she didn't know much about him at all.

Now that was hardly fair, was it?

12

"WHAT ABOUT YOU?" she asked. "Your parents ever try to make you into something you're not?"

His dark gaze glimmered with knowing amusement and he arched a brow. "Deflecting much?" he teased. "If you didn't want to talk about it , you didn't have to. We're all entitled to our secrets," he said, looking away from her. It was a glib comment, but she caught an undercurrent there, one that irrationally made her heart ache for him. He'd said nothing—revealed nothing—and yet she knew he was hiding something painful.

He was the strongest man she'd ever met, with a formidable sense of honor, of duty. A diabolically quick mind. She didn't know what haunted him, but whatever it was had to be substantial to put that kind of expression on his face.

"Who's deflecting now?" she quipped, spearing him with a look.

"What do you want to know?" he asked, humoring her. "I'll answer everything that I want to."

A bark of laughter bubbled from her throat. "Oh, really? Everything that you want to, huh? How thoughtful of you. How open and honest," she drawled, her voice dripping with sarcasm.

His lips twitched with fake modesty. "I try."

She whacked him and heaved a beleaguered breath. "Shut up."

"Are you sure you've never served in our armed forces?" he asked. "Because you bark orders like a pro. And to think you had the nerve to call me autocratic?" He shook his dark head, seemingly baffled at the workings of her twisted female mind.

"Tell you what," she said, an idea forming. "I'll give you carte blanche to ask me anything you want—anything at all—and I will answer truthfully, without being a smart ass, to the best of my ability."

He stopped, seemingly intrigued. "This sounds too good to be true. Let me guess," he said, searching her gaze, his sinfully carnal mouth curving. "You want quid quo pro."

"I do." She nodded once. "We'll take turns. An answer for an answer."

She knew his curiosity was piqued and was trying

to figure out if she'd somehow managed to trick him. He cast another speculative, semi-distrustful glance in her direction, evidently weighing the personal risk of her proposition. "There has to be a limit," he said finally. "Three questions. And each question has to stand on its own. No follow-up questions."

She nodded in agreement. "I agree to your terms. Declare your out-of-bounds," she said.

"Come again?"

"I hope to later, but I'm not talking about sex right now."

His eyes widened in shock, then he laughed again, the sound rich and easy. He should do it more often, Noelle thought. "I w-wasn't either," he told her, his voice breaking with humor. "What do you mean by out-of-bounds?"

"We each name a single topic that is off-limits." She lifted a skeptical brow. "You've never done this before, have you?"

He passed a hand over his face to hide his smile. It didn't work. "No, can't say that I have."

"While you're figuring yours out, I'll tell you mine. My birthday."

Though her grandparents had always tried to make the day special for her, her own parents never had and, ultimately, she'd always wound up hurt and disappointed. As a child she'd actually hated Christmas, resented the baby Jesus for stealing her birthday thunder. She'd outgrown that bit, of course, and had actually started to enjoy Christmas in her late teens, when she'd donned her first apron in a soup kitchen.

Her parents had both been working late, there'd been no special dinner, no traditions, just a few gifts they were going to open the next day. So she'd left the house and found herself downtown. She'd gone into the shelter on a whim…and found her calling.

He frowned, a line furrowing between his dark brows. "Your birthday?"

"That's one," she announced breezily. "And it's out-of-bounds."

"Ha," he said. "Nice try, sweetheart. But we haven't started yet and I haven't told you my off-limits topic."

She feigned exasperation, watched a group of wild turkeys peck their way closer to the creek. "Fine. Go on, then. What it is?"

"My military service."

Wow. She blinked, absorbed that. She should have known that would have been his pick, given the little things that he'd inadvertently revealed, but it was disappointing all the same. Still, she'd made up the rules and she'd have to abide by them. "All right," she said. "I will not ask about your military service."

A little tension leaked out of his frame. "All right.

Ladies first," he said. "Do your worst," he added grimly.

Oh, she would. She was good at this game. "What is the capital of Idaho?"

He opened his mouth, shut it, seemingly stunned. He arched a questioning brow. "Boise."

"Congratulations, you're smarter than a fifth grader." She strolled on, cast a casual look at the darkening sky. "Your turn."

"You're tricking me," he said, his probing gaze searching her face. "I know you are, but I don't know how." He paused, finally shrugged and gave his head a shake. "What is the significance of your tattoo?"

Shit. She should have made that one out-of-bounds. She swallowed. "It's in memory of someone," she admitted. "A child. A little girl name Hope who died as a result of injuries sustained in a tornado in Alabama."

He swore hotly, looked away. "I'm sorry. I had no idea."

She lifted a single shoulder, her heart heavy. "You wouldn't, so no harm done. Most people just think it's a message—and it is—to me. It's a reminder of why I do what I do. Why I ignore my parents and go into recovery zones and ravaged communities. It's why I don't punch a time clock and get accused of not having a real job because I don't actually earn a paycheck," she added bitterly. "But you know what? I don't *need* to earn a paycheck—I'm sure that was in my file—and it's for that very reason I can go where I'm *needed*." The old resentment boiled up in her. "My life isn't measured in how much money I've earned or how much money I haven't—it's measured in doing the next right thing, standing in the gap, helping where help is needed. That's my reward. *That's* my paycheck."

He was smiling at her when she finally stopped ranting and looked up. "Wow," he said. "I like this game."

Noelle grinned self-consciously, felt a blush sting the tops of her ears. "Sorry. I didn't mean to go off on a tangent." Felled by her own sword. Sheesh.

He looked entirely too pleased with himself. "No worries. Your turn."

Noelle studied him from the corner of her eye, let her gaze drift along his jaw, the curve of his lips. He had a gorgeous profile, she thought. Simply breathtaking. "What's the strangest twin connection thing that's ever happened to you?"

He hesitated, shot her a look and groaned. "Oh, hell."

"You've got to answer," she said. "Those were the rules and you didn't call out of bounds."

"I know," he said, rubbing the back of his neck.

He looked like he'd rather cut out his own tongue than answer her, which naturally made her all the more curious.

"This must be really good," she said. "You're wriggling like a worm on a hook."

"It's personal," he said.

"Everything is personal, Judd."

"Yes, but this is different because it says more about him than it does me. It was something that I felt—that manifested," he added significantly, his gaze boring into hers. "But it was as a result of his feelings, you see? His feelings. Not mine." He passed a hand over his face, looked away and swore again. "I haven't even told him," he said. "Because it would embarrass him."

Hmm. "Are you violating the terms of our agreement?"

He arched a hopeful brow. "What's the punishment if I do?"

"Something horrible," she said, her tone dire. "Something truly heinous."

He laughed. "And ambiguous it sounds."

"But worse than that, you'll have to live with the fact that you didn't keep your word."

He winced again, looked away, indecision gnawing at him. "Oh, hell. Fine," he said. "I'll tell you. The first time Judd slept with his wife Sophie, his feelings for her were so…*potent* that I awoke from a dead sleep, oceans away on the island of Crete, with a hard-on."

Noelle felt her eyes nearly bug out of her head. "Seriously?"

"That's another question," he told her. "It pertains to the original and it's not your turn."

He was right, curse him. Another thought struck and she gasped. His text message from his brother, immediately following their vanity sex. Had his brother— Oh, good Lord. Surely not. How mortifying. How miserably embarrassing. How…flattering, she realized. If they shared strong emotion, then that could only mean that he'd really felt something for her. Not just the sex, but *their* sex. She inwardly preened.

He sent her a mistrustful look. "You look too happy," he said grimly.

"Too happy? What a horrible thing to say."

"You know what I mean." And she did.

"Your turn."

He chewed the inside of his cheek, clearly trying to come up with something that was going to throw her. "What are you most looking forward to doing after you testify?"

She opened her mouth to respond and then snapped it shut. "Er…"

"You've got to answer," he said, throwing the rules back at her.

"I know," she said. "I'm thinking. Honestly, I've been so busy just trying to make it to the trial that I haven't given much thought to what I'll do after it."

"I can see where that would be the case. But it still doesn't answer my question."

She struggled, shrugged. "I guess just going home—rebuilding my home," he added significantly.

"Right. The fire," he said. "Was it terribly damaged?"

"Foul," she cried. "You can't ask that."

"Fine," he groused good-naturedly. "But it was an innocent question."

"Maybe so," she told him, shrugging. "But it's my turn."

He grew quiet, waiting.

"Ever been in a serious relationship, engaged or married?"

He turned to look at her, his expression a curious mix of guarded and droll. "That sounds like three questions rolled into one."

"It's not," she argued. "It asks the same thing without allowing you to split hairs."

A muscle worked in his jaw as he tried to find a way to wiggle out of a direct answer. He finally sighed. "Engaged once, which would qualify as a serious relationship, but never married."

Interesting. Had the mystery woman he'd proposed to broken his heart? Noelle wondered, suddenly blindsided with the idea of pummeling the hell out of someone she didn't know and, in all likelihood, would never meet. Jealousy tangled so thoroughly around her heart, she could feel it constricting with rage inside her chest.

"I'm not going to elaborate," he said. "It's ancient history. I was young and stupid. In college," he added. "And she was a miserable conniving bitch who was more interested in my trust fund than me."

She grinned pointedly. "I thought you weren't going to elaborate."

He blinked, then swore. "So that's the trick, huh?"

"It's the need to explain," she told him. "We all need to rationalize."

They strolled on, hand in hand, the sun sinking lower and lower below the mountains. Dusky orange light painted the sky and backlit the trees, making them look like they were on fire. It was nice, Noelle thought. Just being with him like this. Easy, even.

"We'd better start heading back," he said.

She nodded in agreement, then spied a familiar car going over the bridge. She jerked her head in that direction. "Looks like Chad and Marissa are back again," she said. "Doing a repeat of their social experiment."

"Oh, is that what the kids are calling it these days?" he deadpanned.

Noelle chuckled. "I hope they're using protection. Little fools."

"They're young and invincible and smarter than everyone else," he drawled. "Of course, they're not using protection."

"Maybe we should bring them some." She scattered leaves with the tip of her makeshift walking stick. "The Ranger security wives put condoms in my care package."

He drew up short and stared at her. "They *what?*"

Noelle laughed at his incredulous expression. "Oh, dear. Has your honor been called into question?"

"What? No, it's just—"

"Forward thinking," she said. "I mistook you for a stripper when you first walked in and I'm passably attractive. Two hot-blooded single people—one of them newly returned from military service—forced under threat of death into close proximity." She lifted a lazy shoulder. "Alas, the odds were not in our favor."

He slowed, turned to look at her, his expression suddenly flat and unreadable. "So you're saying that either one of us could have been replaced with someone else and had the same outcome?"

She blinked, gasped as realization dawned and shook her head. "God, no. Sorry, that's not what I meant at all. I just meant that, on the surface, it was a reasonable conclusion to make."

"Right." He resumed walking, his face still blank, his lips compressed. Was he jealous? she wondered. Or were his feelings merely hurt because he suspected he might not have had the magical penis to end all penises? Either way, his feelings were obviously hurt, and it made her feel awful.

She tugged at his hand, forcing him to slow. "Judd, really. That came out wrong. That's not what I meant at all. Today was—" She wracked her brain for the right words. "You are—" She swore. Dammit, this was hard. "Today was special. Unmatched," she added softly. "Better than any other day ever. Ever," she repeated. "Couldn't you tell?" she asked smally, feeling her face heat.

A slow grin drifted lazily across his face. "You're blushing."

"It happens occasionally," she conceded. "You've got one question left," she reminded him. "Or had you forgotten?"

"I hadn't forgotten. I'm merely biding my time. You didn't mention an expiration date on my remaining question. I can save it, right?"

She winced, hesitated. "I'd rather you didn't," she

hedged. It was a brilliant strategy. She wished she'd thought of it.

"Is it against the rules?"

"No."

He squeezed her hand. "Then I'm going to hold on to it for a while longer. Who knows what I might need to know later?"

She sighed heavily. Who knew, indeed?

"I bet you feel like kicking yourself," he remarked, a self-satisfied smile sliding over his lips.

"I feel like kicking *you,*" she said. "It's taking an enormous amount of energy to refrain."

Their cabin loomed into view, the porch lights ablaze from the front. Lilo and Stitch were sitting side by side in the window, patiently waiting for their return.

"Look," he drawled. "Your tiny cats are glaring at us."

She chuckled. "They're not glaring," she chided. "They're looking. And they're tiny because they're dwarves," she added. "They can't help their size any more than you can help yours." They'd been a little standoffish to Judd and, though she'd never admit it to him, there was something a little unnerving about their unblinking stares. It made her wonder what they thought. What they could see.

His eyebrows climbed his forehead. "Dwarves?"

"Yes. I'd suspected when I got them, but my vet confirmed it a few weeks ago. They're not going to get much bigger. Well, their legs and paws, anyway. Their bodies might grow a little more."

"Wow," he said, allowing her to mount the steps ahead of him. "I've never heard of that before."

"It's rare, though there are breeders who purposely try to encourage the condition."

He grimaced as he opened the door. "That's horrible."

"I know." Lilo and Stitch bounded over, yowled loudly and curled around her legs. "Evidently there is a profit in it."

"Dwarves," he repeated, chuckling softly under his breath. He glanced up, caught her stare. "I guess that makes you Snow White after all."

She blinked. "Come again?"

His expression suddenly changed and a predatory light glinted in his black eyes, making a thrill whip through her. She knew that look and so did the rest of her. Her belly quivered and need ballooned inside of her, stealing her breath as she met his gaze.

"You bet," he promised. "Right now." Then he stepped forward and slung her over his shoulder once again, making her squeal in delight in the process, then bounded up the stairs.

"How do you feel about taking a bath?" he asked.

Her pulse leapt in her veins. Him, naked and wet. Hers to explore, to taste. To slip and slide all over.

"Depends," she said. "Are we going to get dirty before or after?"

"During," he said. "And I've hidden all the towels."

13

JUDD'S BOOTED FOOT had no sooner hit the last step when his cell phone went off. He carefully plopped Noelle onto the bed, then quickly grabbed the device from his waist.

Payne.

He glanced at Noelle, who was watching nervously, before answering. "Anderson," he said by way of greeting.

"Judd, I have news," he said.

He winced. Braced himself. "Is it good?"

"It is for your client. D.A. Stark got the trial date moved up. She testifies day after tomorrow. Friday."

Judd stilled. "Friday?"

"That's right."

"You'll do the official hand-off at 8:00 a.m. on Friday morning. I'd suggest moving into a location closer to Mossy Ridge ahead of time to lessen your drive, but since you've avoided detection I think it would be better to wait. Perhaps Ms. Montgomery wouldn't mind taking a nap in the car on the way in while you drive."

Judd knew he was new to the security business, but something about that plan rang false. Unnecessary, even. His spidey senses tingled. "Is there more?" he asked.

A simple, but effective way to get to the truth.

"As it happens, yes, " Payne said, his voice guarded. "Are you alone?"

"Not at the moment, no."

"Then be careful how you respond and I'll leave the dissemination of information to you. I've had an odd call here. Someone claiming to be an assistant of Ed Johnson's wanted a status briefing on this case. This person wanted the contact information of the agent in charge."

Judd swore. He knew for a fact that Ed trusted no one, that he'd made it quite clear that he and he alone was the only person who was supposed to be regularly informed on this case and that his contact would be limited to avoid an unnecessary mistake which might result in a "poor outcome"—as in dead—for Noelle.

His gaze inexplicably slid to where she sat perched

on the bed. She'd pulled her shoes off, scooted back against the headboard and had drawn her knees up to her chest and wrapped her arms around them. Lilo and Stitch gamboled around her, batting at a long curly strand of her fiery hair.

An odd pain winged through his chest as he looked at her, swelled to the point he could barely speak. He cleared his throat. "Have you been able to ID the caller?"

"Not yet," Payne admitted. "Naturally, he gave a false name, but the phone software pinged it as a Mossy Ridge number."

"And what does Ed say?"

"Ed's livid. He says he told no one who he hired, not even his wife. He's rattled that the information has been compromised."

Understandably so, Judd thought.

"This caller was smooth, Judd. Had I not known exactly what we were dealing with here, I might have believed him. He was that good. And the further into the conversation we got, when it became increasingly clear that he wasn't going to get the information he wanted, he became frantic and irrational."

Judd's eyes narrowed fractionally, then he jerked his head toward the door, indicating that he'd take the rest of the call in private, before leaving the room and lowering his voice. "You think it's the same guy who has been after her all along?"

They'd suspected that a single man had been responsible for the attacks on her life, simply because had two people been working on it, they might have succeeded already. They'd also suspected it was an amateur at work, for the very same reason. This fit.

"I do," he said. "And this guy isn't a natural born killer. He sounds like a desperate soccer dad who owes the wrong people, is above suspicion and over a barrel."

Judd swore, looked out the floor-to-ceiling windows and watched the last of the sun slip below the horizon. He pinched the bridge of his nose. "Desperate men are unpredictable."

Payne concurred. "And dangerous. This could be anybody, Judd. *Anybody.* My guess is that this is someone Noelle knows, might even trust. If she saw this person, she'd never assume that he meant her harm."

"Are we certain we trust Stark?" Judd asked. "Because I don't want to do the transfer at the last minute for the D.A. to screw this up and get her killed." He didn't want to let her out of his sight. He wanted to wrap her in Kevlar and personally escort her into the courthouse, then vet every person who came into the courtroom himself.

And what was supposed to happen post trial? After her testimony? This entire time they'd all been laboring under the assumption that she'd be safe once she'd given her testimony, that there would be no benefit to her death afterward because the damage would have been done.

But this was Tubby Winchester. He was a damned nut with a vindictive streak a mile wide—hell, he'd killed Rupert Nichols because the man had refused to stock his favorite ketchup. A sickening feeling of dread invaded his belly.

She'd never be safe, Judd thought. Even with Tubby behind bars, without some other form of protection, without some other form of resolution, she'd always be ducking and hiding, always looking over her shoulder.

It was a damned shitty way to live.

"Every bit of information I have on Stark suggests that he hasn't misrepresented himself at all. He's been waiting for years for a slam dunk case to take Tubby out of the picture. He's certain that if he takes the head—Tubby, I mean—then the rest of his crime body will twitch for a little while, but ultimately die."

That made sense, he supposed. Still…"I don't want to hand her off," Judd told him. "I want to do the escort personally."

Silence stretched across the line while Payne presumably mulled that telling statement over. He'd just tipped his hand, but so what? He couldn't let her go, not when he needed to be there to protect her. "I think that's for the best. I'll alert Stark."

"One day of testimony, right?"

"Provided the defense finishes with her," Payne told him.

"They'd better," he said grimly. Because he was taking her the hell out of there the minute she finished. He didn't know where, he didn't know how, really, at this point. He just knew that she wasn't going to be safe—permanently safe, anyway—until he could mine a solution from his suddenly seizing brain to make her that way.

"I'm assuming you've inspected your weapon," Payne remarked levelly. He was aware, of course, of the true reason he'd left the military.

"I have," he said. "And, should the need to use it become essential, then I'm confident I can carry out my duty to our client." And he was. He'd been hired to protect her, dammit.

"I never doubted it," Payne told him.

Then that made one of them, Judd thought, swallowing at the vote of confidence. He'd been relatively certain that he could pick up a gun, aim and fire it if he had to on her behalf, but a sliver of doubt had remained in the back of his mind, a taunting reminder of his previous inability to do so.

Not anymore.

He'd pick off anyone who threatened her, Judd thought. Without a second thought or a moment's hesitation. He knew it. Felt the resolve firmly in his fingers.

"Keep me posted," he said. "I've got this."

Payne agreed, then disconnected. He turned then to go back into the bedroom and saw Noelle standing in the bedroom doorway. He heaved a sigh. He should have known that she wouldn't sit still, that she'd want to listen in.

It was her life on the line, after all. He could hardly fault her for that.

"What's happening?" she asked, her ordinarily animated face a mask of worry.

He brought her fully up to speed, leaving nothing out. She'd been so brave, he thought. His Christmas angel. His Snow White. His intergalactic princess. God, had he ever met anyone so remarkable? Anyone so good but so capable of being wicked? Had he ever met anyone who cared so much about the world and the people in it? So determined to make a difference, with no thought to personal gain.

No, he hadn't. And he instinctively knew he never

would again. She was singular, unique. One of a kind. His to protect.

She worried her bottom lip, seemed to absorb everything and filter it through that remarkable brain. "I always imagined that it was someone I knew," she said. "But it never occurred to me that they were being coerced into action, forced to kill me."

"Does that make a difference?"

"Yes, it does," she said. "It changes the motive. This man is obviously trying to protect someone— more than likely his family—and has been backed into a corner. He bears me no ill will, no grudge. He's not crazy or cruel. He's desperate. And desperation is something I understand." She lifted a slim shoulder. "I see it all the time when I'm working relief. People will do the unthinkable when they feel like they don't have any choice."

That was true, he knew. Still… "He's been trying to *kill* you, Noelle. He doesn't get a pass because he has his reasons, no matter how good they might be."

"I'm not giving him a pass," she said. "Just a little grace."

He shook his head, marveling at her. "Then you're a better person than I am."

"No, I'm not," she told him. "More highly evolved, maybe," she teased, the familiar light returning to her lovely green eyes.

A bark of laughter erupted from his throat. "More highly evolved, eh?"

She sidled forward, wrapped her arms around his middle and settled her head on his chest. "Thank you," she murmured, startling him.

"For what?"

"For caring," she said simply. "I heard you ask to take me to the courthouse. I figured you'd be thrilled to get rid of me. I never expected you to ask for additional duty."

He swallowed, his throat clogged with emotion. "You've grown on me," he said gruffly. Truer words had never been spoken. Never more terrifying either, but there it was.

"I've got an idea," she told him, leaning up to kiss the side of his neck. A shudder wracked through him. "Why don't you grow *inside* of me?"

HOURS LATER, nestled in the sex tub, as Judd liked to call it, Noelle settled against his chest, between the V of his legs, and ate the chocolate candies from the honeymoon basket. The scent of honeysuckle massage oil and sex perfumed the air and the feather lay forgotten on the bed, but the ways he'd used it never would be.

Mercy.

Who knew something so soft and delicate could

illict such evocative feelings, could make her shiver and quake with a single sweep of it across her abdomen. There'd been a frantic edge to their lovemaking after he'd talked to his boss, Noelle had noted. Almost as though he'd needed to control her—control them—to keep the rest of the world in line.

She understood perfectly.

And she'd been happy to let him do it, to let him boss her around, to take her hard and fast. He'd needed the release and she'd needed...him. It was an alarming development she should have anticipated, but didn't. Though she'd like to chalk these extraordinary feelings up to dire circumstances or even Stockholm syndrome, she thought with an inward chuckle, she knew that wasn't the case.

It was him. *Judd.* Even his name stirred something deep inside of her. It made her organs clench in recognition, made her stomach drop and her breasts tingle. She didn't know what it was about him, what specifically it was that made him so damned remarkable— aside from his criminal handsomeness and massive sex appeal, she thought—that made him the one who just ultimately...did it for her.

Was she in love with him? Could she be in love with him after so short a time? It was possible, she supposed. She knew it had happened for other people. But if this wasn't love, then it was some variety thereof. She cared for him—deeply, given the ache in her chest the minute she'd realized their expiration date had arrived early—felt an overwhelming affection for him, one that she'd never experienced for anyone else before.

And when it came to sex…

Her womb clenched in remembered pleasure and she squirmed against him, felt him stir at her back. Heat moved through her, wound through her limbs and concentrated in her lady bits. Sizzled in anticipation of his touch, of his lips on her skin, his hands on her body, stroking, kneading, enflaming.

She reached up behind her, turned her head and brought his down for her kiss. His lips were soft, but firm, skilled. Though she could feel the tension climbing in his touch, he was unhurried, determined to enjoy the way their mouths moved together. She suckled his tongue, drawing it deeper into her mouth and felt him nudge harder up against her.

His big hands slipped around her, one at her breasts, toying with an achy nipple, the other sliding between her legs, where he put the palm of his hand flat against her sex and applied the perfect amount of pressure.

She groaned into his mouth, wiggled against him, need impossibly welling again. Every time she thought she was incapable of having another orgasm, he proved her wrong, like it was some sort of test he had to pass, a point he had to prove.

Lucky her, Noelle thought. He could score and score and score as far as she was concerned. Hell, this was a game she'd gladly forfeit if it meant she could keep having him, keep feeling him deep inside of her.

She turned then and straddled him, settled her nether lips over the long ridge of his arousal, making sensation whip through her. She winced with pleasure, sucking air through her teeth.

"I love that little sound you make," he told her, his voice low and gruff with need. "It makes me so friggin' *hot*," he said, coupling the world with a deliberate stroke against her clit.

"You know what makes me hot?" she asked, emboldened by his compliment.

"Tell me," he growled, his big hands sliding over her back and settling on her hips as she undulated over him, not quite taking him in, biding her time, building his anticipation. "Shock me." He chuckled. "You routinely do."

She drew back and looked at him. "Really? I shock you? Little ole me?" She shook her head. "You must keep boring company."

"Not true," he insisted, shifting at her entrance, trying to come inside of her.

She evaded him, slid back and pressed a kiss onto

his chest, flicked her tongue against his male nipple. His gorgeous skin gleamed in the light, wet and slippery, his dark hair pushed away from his face. And his eyes—God, help her, those eyes—burned with desire and something else, something she didn't quite recognize but knew was significant all the same.

"You're remarkable, Noelle," he told her. "The most interesting person I've ever met."

She laughed softly. "Interesting like a science experiment or interesting as exotic and mysterious?"

"Definitely the latter," he told her, a smile in his voice. He snorted. "A science experiment," he repeated. "Your mind must be a really interesting place to live."

"It is," she told him, settling onto the head of his penis, taking a little bit of him in, but not seating herself firmly onto him. It took every bit of strength she possessed to hold herself steady, to resist.

She wanted him to snap. She loved pushing him past his breaking point, making him mindless with need, with want for her. Only her.

With a low growl, gratifyingly, he did.

At last, hallelujah, amen.

"Enough," he said, then reached over and turned on the jets, making the tub bubble and roil. In less than a heartbeat, he'd rolled her onto her side and slid right into her. She inhaled sharply from the invasion, felt him nudge her core, her muscles clench. She clung to the side of the tub, held on while he stroked her intimately, long and deep.

"I wish you could know how good this feels," she said, her voice broken, raw. "I wish you could feel what I'm feeling, how much I love the way you move inside of me. Every vein and ridge, every perfect inch."

He laughed darkly. "Oh, I think I've got a vague idea," he told her, flexing deep, growing impossibly harder.

"You might," she said, laughing softly as pleasure built in her sex, the heat building, feeding on itself.

Judd slipped farther under her, then lifted her leg and anchored it on the side of the tub. "I'm going to try something," he said. "Do you trust me?"

"Unequivocally." And she did, she realized. Completely. She didn't know if this meant she'd achieved some level of unprecedented insightfulness or if she'd just lost her mind. She smothered a hysterical laugh.

Probably both.

"All right," he said, sliding her body down the side of the big tub until—

"Oh!"

"There it is." He chuckled. "Brace yourself, sweetheart. This is going to be good."

The hot stream of water firing from the jets

pounded her clit while he pistoned in and out of her, a double whammy of sensation that made her entire body hum with so much sensation she was surprised she didn't just light up from the glow.

Her breath came in little hard puffs, her hands bit into the side of tub as she held on for dear life. It was almost too much. Too good. He stretched her, filled her, the hot water pounding relentlessly at her from the front, his dick buried deep inside of her, pounding from behind…

She felt the orgasm well up inside of her, reach an unmatched crescendo, then she exploded. Fractured. Flew into a million pieces.

Which was odd considering her body bowed so hard from the shock of it that she went teeth-clenchingly rigid, every muscle atrophied with joy, with unparalleled bliss.

She felt Judd jerk from behind, heard a guttural growl rip from his throat, felt him spasm inside of her. Her dark angel, her protector, her…

Hers.

Breathing raggedly, he pressed a kiss to her temple while his dick remained buried deep and twitching with the aftermath of his orgasm. Or maybe it was hers, she thought. Either way, the feeling was indescribably perfect. Beautiful.

"I'm not going to let anyone hurt you, Noelle," he said. "Ever."

The promise burrowed into her heart, made tears prick the backs of her eyes. "I'm not going to let anyone hurt you either," she said. *Even yourself,* she silently added. Because she suspected whatever haunted Judd Anderson was a demon he'd created, even fed.

He laughed softly. "You're going to protect me?"

She nodded once. "Damn straight."

Because she suspected he needed a hero as much as she did.

14

CURTIS RETURNED THE phone to the cradle on Thursday morning—his last day to save his family—and felt hysteria fraying the edges of his sanity. His wife had called to remind him of his girls' dance recital this evening—seven o'clock, don't forget!—and in the same breath mentioned that her mother and father weren't going to be able to attend, that her father had gotten some disturbing news.

That was worrisome. Had the man at Ranger Security somehow managed to learn his identity? Curtis wondered. He'd taken precautions before making the call. He'd bought a disposable phone, had kept the conversation to less than a minute and a half to avoid any GPS detection on their end, then had tossed the phone into the man-made pond in their local park once he'd finished with it. And he hadn't given the agent his real name, of course. Still…

Time was running out and every tick of the clock made him a little more sick to his stomach, a little more desperate. He'd considered packing Carla and the kids up and simply leaving town, but even though he'd gone through the house and removed the multiple bugs and mini-cameras, he couldn't be certain that he'd gotten them all, that he wouldn't tip his hand and get them all killed for their trouble.

It was tempting though, because if he couldn't find out where Noelle Montgomery was, then they were all dead anyway. A little sob welled in his throat and he hung his head, massaged his temples.

An email arrived in his inbox with a ding, reminding him that he was at work—where he was expected to pretend like his life didn't hang in the balance—so in absence of a better plan, he tried to focus on what he could control. What he *could* do.

The email was one of those viral video links from an unknown sender, but the subject line grabbed his attention. "The break you needed. Don't fuck it up."

Heart pounding, he slid his mouse over the link and clicked. "Hi, I'm Chad," a boy in his midtwenties announced at the beginning. "And I'm Marissa," his companion said. "We're sociology majors at the University of Tennessee and if you're watching this video, then you, too, are contributing to our social experiment."

Curtis frowned. Social experiment? How was this the break he needed? How did this couple pretending to be stranded motorists who were running an informal poll to see who would stop and offer assistance pertain to his problem? He'd just about convinced himself that he'd read the message wrong, that it hadn't come from Team Tubby, as he'd begun to call it, when a couple rolled into view on screen. "This sweet couple was our last passersby," the girl said. "And they proved me right," she added. "They initially drove past, but then turned around and came back, which put me ahead in the society-isn't-doomed-from-indifference category." She jabbed a little victory fist in the air. "Win!"

Curtis leaned forward, felt his jaw go slack. *Noelle Montgomery.* In the passenger seat. Sweet Lord…

"This kind couple not only expressed concern over our being on the side of the road, but admonished us for setting up shop there in the first place and advised us to move to a safer locale. See?" the girl said. "There's hope for us yet."

Yes, Curtis thought, there was.

It took twenty minutes to locate the pair, convince them that he was an executive with a popular reality TV show and wanted to interview them for a potential spot on the next season. They'd been eager to share, thrilled to reveal every last detail about their experiment, including the exact location where the video was filmed. He didn't have an address, but he had a road and a good look at the vehicle.

He had to do it, Curtis thought, nausea burning the back of his throat. He didn't have a choice.

THIS WAS A bad idea, Judd thought, following Noelle along the creek once again. He should have never agreed to let her out of the house, never allowed her to wheedle him into putting them out in the open like this. Granted, he didn't think they'd been compromised—he couldn't imagine how—but he couldn't deny the tension tightening his gut, couldn't ignore the finger of unease prodding his belly. It had been so bad that his brother had sent him a text, one that simply contained a question mark.

Hell if he knew, Judd thought. He didn't have any of the answers. In fact, right now, he'd definitely say that he had more questions than answers. As such, he'd called Payne early this morning and shared a few of his concerns.

"She's never going to be safe," he'd told him. "Even if Tubby goes to jail, he's going to send someone after her."

"It's possible," Payne had agreed. "But even if she

backed out now and didn't testify, it wouldn't change anything. She's too much of a liability."

And he'd been right. Judd had considered trying to talk her out of giving her testimony, then had decided he'd have a better chance of telling the mountain their cabin sat on to move to Portugal.

None.

She'd come this far, she was doing the right thing, had sacrificed enough already. And he admired her for that resolve, he really did. Noelle Montgomery had honor. It was an antiquated notion, but he liked it. He admired her for it. Particularly after she'd shared the details of what had happened, how the murder had affected her. And it also explained why she was so devoted to those cats. "I don't know what I'll do with them the next time I need to go into the field," she said. "But they're mine. I can't give them up."

To his astonishment, he'd offered to keep them for her. The smile she'd given him after that was nothing short of wondering, had made him feel more like a hero than anything else he'd ever done.

He'd also committed himself to her beyond this mission.

She'd recognized the significance, then leaned forward and kissed him. They'd kissed a lot over the past couple of days—and more, so much more, he thought, his balls tightening—but that kiss…that kiss had been an earmark. It had signaled a change.

He'd called his brother directly after and asked him if he and Noelle could come there once she'd testified, just until he could figure something out, some way to thwart Tubby. Sophie, having had her own troubles, had practically built a fortress around her farm. It was the safest place he knew of. Nothing would come over that wall.

He hadn't mentioned it to Noelle yet. He was biding his time, waiting until the right moment.

"You're awfully quiet," she said. "And grim-looking. What's wrong?"

"I don't like being out here," he said. "We're too exposed."

"No one knows we're here."

"Doesn't matter," he said, shaking his head.

She paused to look at him. "Is this a gut feeling or are you being paranoid. Be honest."

"I'm always honest."

"You evade," she said.

He arched a brow. "And you don't?"

She merely grinned at him, tucked a long strand of that gorgeous hair behind the delicate shell of her ear. "I'm cautious," she said. "There's a difference."

"It must be damned subtle."

"It is," she said. "I'm not surprised that you're confused."

He grinned and gritted his teeth. "You know, half the time I'm with you I'm either thinking about tumbling you onto your back or throttling you. Sometimes I'm thinking about both. It's damned confusing."

She tsked. "Sex and violence often go hand and hand."

"Like now," he growled. "Now is a perfect example."

She threaded her fingers through his, gave his hand a squeeze. "You never answered me," she prompted.

It took him a second to sift through the threads of their conversation. Oh, yeah. "It's a gut feeling," he said. "One my brother shares and his instincts are far better than mine."

She chuckled darkly. "I doubt that very seriously."

"You've never met him."

"I don't have to. I trust you. *You,*" she repeated. "And if you say we should go back, then we will."

"You're being remarkable agreeable," he noted, somewhat distrustfully. "Should I be worried?"

She chewed the inside of her cheek. "I was hoping you'd be flattered."

"I am." Which reminded him… "I made a few calls this morning and, if it's all right with you, I'd like for you to come back to my brother and sister-in-law's place and stay there for a while after you're finished in court."

She frowned, a line emerging between her brows. "A while? Define a while."

"Until I can be sure that none of Tubby's people are going to harm you," he said. "So what that really means is…I don't know. But I don't want you to—"

"Yes," she said, a smile lighting her face, her raspberry mouth heartbreakingly happy.

"It would mean spending your birthday with me and my family. Is that all right?" She hadn't mentioned any plans, but that didn't mean she didn't have any.

An odd expression passed over her face. "Christmas, you mean."

"What?"

"You said I'd be spending my birthday with your family. Didn't you mean Christmas?"

He blinked. "Isn't your birthday December 25th?"

"It is. Christmas day."

He lifted his shoulder. "Maybe so, but that's not what makes it special for you, is it?"

Or him either, from now on, he suspected. It would always be about Noelle. He'd never see an ornament or hear a Christmas carol again without thinking of her.

Another one of those smiles tugged at her lips. "That's right. I'm just not used to anyone making a big deal over it," she finally admitted.

He squeezed her hand, emotion rushing though him. "This year is going to be different."

"It already has been," she said softly. Something caught her attention in the distance and she frowned. "That looks like—"

He followed her gaze, spied a person on their front porch. "Marissa," he finished. "What's she doing out here?"

"I don't know," she muttered, hurrying forward. "But Chad's not with her. I hope nothing is wrong."

Judd's cell vibrated at his waist and he grabbed it and held it up to his ear as he trailed after her. "Anderson," he said.

"You've been compromised," Payne said. "Get her out of there now."

He blinked, stunned. "Compromised? How?"

"A couple you stopped to offer assistance to posted a video online and it's gone viral. Evidently they were doing a social experiment of some sort and used a hidden camera."

Judd's gaze flew to Marissa, whose ashen expression was terrified. "Noelle!" he shouted. "Stop."

A shot rang out from beside the house, clipping the dirt right in front of her feet. She screamed and dropped to her knees, but not before a questioning "Curtis?" left her lips.

Judd spotted the shooter, quickly pulled the weapon from the band in the back of his jeans and leveled it at him. His finger was dead certain on the trigger and he'd begun to squeeze when Noelle screamed at him.

"No, Judd! Please, don't! Don't kill him! Don't become a murderer because of me!"

A black rage had descended over his brain and he kept pressing forward, getting a better bead on Curtis, who was cowering like a sniveling little worm at the corner of the house. He clearly didn't have any idea how to shoot a gun, but incompetent fools often shot people accidentally.

And he'd shot at her—on Judd's watch.

He laughed darkly. "No worries on that score, sweetheart. I'm already a murderer. Hundreds of times over. I was a sniper," he admitted. "Nicknamed the Angel of Death I was so damned good at my job."

"That's not murder," she said. "That's strategic warfare. There's a difference."

"Really?" he asked. "Do you really think so? Because I don't. Not anymore."

"You followed orders," she insisted. "You did what you were told to do in order to preserve the peace, to save lives. Thank you," she said. "Thank you for doing the hard job, the one that no one else wants, the one that takes more courage and strength of conviction than any other. Thank you, Judd, from the bottom of my heart. It couldn't have been easy and yet, you did it. Are you listening, Curtis? Take note," she said, her voice cracking. "Because *this* is the way a man behaves."

"I'm sorry, Noelle!" Curtis wailed brokenly. "They're going to kill my family. Cut up my little girls. R-rape my wife," he sobbed. "They still are, if you're not dead today. If I don't kill you."

"Well, you aren't going to kill me, Curtis," she said, perfectly reasonably.

Judd's eyes threatened to leave their sockets.

Marissa whimpered from the front porch.

Curtis blinked drunkenly, as though he didn't know quite what to make of her either. "I have to," he said.

"No, you don't, Curtis. Judd, here, is going to shoot you if you try to shoot me again and, let's just be honest here, you're not a very good hit man," she told him, pity coloring her tone. "And that's because you're not a killer, Curtis. Do you understand? You aren't wired for this sort of behavior. You are not like Tubby Winchester."

"I know that," he said, his eyes frantic. "You think I don't know that? But my family. I'll—"

"Your family will be perfectly safe," she insisted with so much authority that even Judd was inclined to believe her. "Judd is going to call and arrange for their immediate entry into protective custody."

That was news to him, Judd thought.

"They're watching me, watching the house. They'll know."

"There are ways around that. These men are professionals, you understand. They can fix this."

He shook his head, but a hopeful glint lit his gaze. "Do you think so?"

"I do," she said. "But you're going to have to be brave for your family, Curtis. You're going to have to own up to your mistakes, no matter how terrible they are. Do you understand?"

He nodded jerkily.

"You can't let these bastards win, Curtis. You can't let them bully you and hurt your family. It's time for you to be the man Carla married, the father Breanne and Caro deserve. Good men make bad decisions all the time. It's how you react to those decisions that sets you apart."

She was really good at this, Judd thought. She knew exactly what to say to get through to Curtis. She kept reminding him of their connection, referring to the familiar, appealing to a lost sense of honor. And it was working.

But Judd still wanted to kill him.

"I'm sorry, Noelle," Curtis said, weeping quietly, a broken man. "So sorry, for everything."

"You haven't done anything yet that can't be undone, Curtis. Let us help you," she implored. "Please."

Curtis looked at Judd, fire and desperation in his wet eyes. "Can you really go get my family? Can you really put them somewhere safe until I can fix this?"

Judd certainly knew what that felt like. He had his own problems to fix. His own person to protect. "I can," he said. "With a single phone call I can get an extraction team to your house and have your family safely hustled out of there before anyone knows what's happened."

Curtis nodded, dropped the weapon, defeated. "Do it," he said. "And I'll do whatever I have to in order to make things right."

"So you're not a producer from *Terror Train?*" Marissa asked, looking on at Curtis in obvious confusion. "This wasn't a trial run to see if I could qualify?"

Curtis blinked. "No, sorry."

Judd unclipped his cell phone to make the call for Curtis, but it vibrated in his hand. He checked the display and answered. It was Payne again.

"Tubby Winchester was found murdered in his cell a few minutes ago," he said. "Someone shivved him."

Shock burst through him. "Any idea who?"

"The surveillance feed malfunctioned."

"That's convenient."

"It's expedient, if nothing else. I guess he had enemies everywhere, including jail. It's a lucky break, but we'll take it."

Judd glanced at Noelle, at Curtis. Well, the head was officially off the animal, so to speak. Permanently. Which meant that they'd be safe, Judd thought. It was over.

"I'll let them know. I'm assuming the trial is cancelled?"

"Them?" Payne asked. "Who is them?"

"Noelle," he said. "And the guy who has been trying to kill her. She's talked him out of it, and I was just about to call you and arrange for protection for his family."

"She talked him out of it?" Payne parroted, his voice cracking with humor. "I would have liked to see that."

He glanced at Noelle, felt his chest constrict. "It was quite a show."

"I'll just bet it was."

Judd disconnected and told them the news. "It's over."

Noelle's face blanked and she went perfectly still. "Over? Really?"

Curtis collapsed to the ground, relief pouring out of him. "I can't believe it," he said. "I can't believe it's really over."

He couldn't either, Judd thought. And as happy as he was for Noelle's safety, he was painfully aware that she wouldn't need him anymore. And he hadn't realized how much her needing him had meant to him until just now.

NOELLE WATCHED AS Curtis was reunited with his family at the police department, where he'd gone to confess his part in Tubby's crooked business and then turned to look at Judd. It was past dark, the Christmas lights blinking merrily along the city sidewalk. Mistletoe hung from various lamp posts so that young lovers could stop for a quick kiss and children pointed out items they wanted in store display windows. Mossy Ridge was a sweet little town, but she sincerely doubted she'd ever truly feel safe here again.

Especially after knowing what being truly safe and protected felt like. And, unhappily, as it happened, her protector didn't have any reason to keep protecting her anymore.

She'd looked forward to spending her birthday with him, to meeting his family, to seeing the farm and the spot where he hoped to build his house. He had offered to keep Lilo and Stitch for her, so she knew he wasn't completely walking out of her life, but it certainly felt like it. As far as she knew, her parents still didn't have any idea that she'd nearly been killed several times or that her house had been set on fire.

No holiday again with them obviously.

No worries, Noelle told herself. She'd volunteer to serve food and help hand out presents at the local Help center. Maybe she'd look for another mission trip. She could find something to do. She always did.

"Well," Judd announced, his hesitant gaze searching hers. "I'm glad that Curtis kept his word and manned up," he told her. "I was a little worried that he might not."

"He'd been looking for the opportunity to do the right thing," she said. "He was just too worried to see it. Too afraid for his family."

"But you saw it."

Her gaze tangled significantly with his. "I see a lot of things." She quirked a brow, studying him. "For instance, do you know what I see when I look at you?"

"I'm afraid to ask," he said, his eyes guarded.

"You don't have to ask because I'm going to tell you anyway."

He snorted. "I figured as much."

"I see a really good-looking man," she said. "One who is, like it or not, beautiful. Hot and sexy," she added. "I see a man with a smile that melts my insides, a man whose first instinct is never for himself. I see a man who does his job—whatever that might be, however difficult it might be," she said significantly. "And I see a man who'd had enough and decided a change was in order. I see a brave man."

I see a man I could fall in love with, Noelle added silently.

He stared at her, those probing dark eyes rife with tension, emotion. "You see too much," he said. "You scare the hell out of me."

"You scare the hell out of me, too," she said. "But I'm not running. I'm going to be brave. Because I can be scared without being a coward," she said, throwing his words back at him.

He chuckled softly. "Are you suggesting I'm not brave? That I'm being a coward?"

"I'll tell you later, when this conversation is over."

He looked away, shifted his feet, as though summoning the courage to tell her something. It made her ache, seeing him struggle. But it was necessary if they were going to move forward. Noelle didn't expect a happily ever after at this point—it was too soon for that, even if she strongly suspected that was going to be the case—but she was willing to take a bet on the potential of one.

"And what if I don't want the conversation to be

over?" he finally asked. "What if I want to keep talking to you?"

Noelle felt a grin tug at the corner of her mouth, the beginnings of joy spreading through her. "I would love that," she admitted. "And if we continued the conversation in a bathtub, then all the better."

His eyes darkened and a darker chuckle bubbled up his throat. "I've got one question left, remember?"

She nodded, albeit a little anxiously. "I do."

"Would you still come to the farm and spend your birthday with me?" he asked. "I'd love for you to meet my family. And you can bring Lilo and Stitch. It's a farm, after all. I know no one would object."

Happiness and joy swirled inside of her, making her middle warm and fizzy. "I'd be honored," she said. "And since I'm essentially homeless at the moment, your invitation is well-timed."

"And well-received?"

She looped her arms around his neck, pressed a kiss beneath his jaw, breathing him in. "Very well-received."

* * * * *

#729 THE RISK-TAKER · *Uniformly Hot!*
by Kira Sinclair

Returned POW Gage Harper is no hero. He blames himself
for his team's capture in Afghanistan, and the last thing he
wants is to relive his story. But journalist Hope Rawlings,
the girl he could never have, is willing to do anything to get
it. Gage just might be her ticket out of Sweetheart, South
Carolina—and what a hot ticket he is!

#730 LYING IN BED · *The Wrong Bed*
by Jo Leigh

Right bed...wrong woman. When FBI agent Ryan Vail goes
undercover at a ritzy resort to investigate a financial scam
at an intimacy retreat for couples, he'll have to call on all
his skills. Like pretending to be in love with his "wife," aka
fellow agent Angie Wolf. Problem is he and sexy Angie
had a near fling months ago, and now the heat is definitely
on while they share a hotel room—and a bed. Can they
get through all those grueling intimacy exercises, all that
touching and caressing...without giving the game away?

#731 HIS KIND OF TROUBLE · *The Berringers*
by Samantha Hunter

Bodyguard Chance Berringer must tame the feisty celebrity
chef Ana Perez to protect her, but the heat between them
is unstoppable, and so may be the danger.... Ana dismisses
the threats at every turn, but she can't dismiss Chance
or their incredible sexual chemistry. Soon the boundary
between personal and professional is so blurred that
Chance must make the hardest decision of all....

#732 ONE MORE KISS
by Katherine Garbera

When a whirlwind Vegas courtship goes bust,
Alysse Dresden realizes she has to pick up the pieces
and move on. Now, years later, her ex insists he'll win her
back! Though she's curious about what's changed his mind,
Alysse is reluctant to give her heart another chance, not to
mention Jay Cutler. Still, she can't deny he's the one man
she's never forgotten.

#733 RELENTLESS SEDUCTION
by Jillian Burns

A girls' weekend in New Orleans sounds like the breakout
event Claire Brooks has been waiting for. But when her
friend goes missing, Claire, who's always been on the
straight and narrow, admits she needs the help of local
Rafe Moreau, a mysterious loner. Rafe's raw sensuality
tempts Claire like no other...and she can't say no!

#734 THE WEDDING FLING
by Meg Maguire

Tabloid-shy actress Leigh Bailey has always avoided scandal.
But she's bound to make the front page when she escapes on
a tropical honeymoon getaway—without her groom! Lucky her
hunky pilot Will Burgess is there to make sure she doesn't get
too lonely....

HBCNM1212ENHREVB1

REQUEST YOUR FREE BOOKS!
2 FREE NOVELS PLUS 2 FREE GIFTS!

red-hot reads!

YES! Please send me 2 FREE Harlequin® Blaze™ novels and my 2 FREE gifts (gifts are worth about $10). After receiving them, if I don't wish to receive any more books, I can return the shipping statement marked "cancel." If I don't cancel, I will receive 6 brand-new novels every month and be billed just $4.49 per book in the U.S. or $4.96 per book in Canada. That's a saving of at least 14% off the cover price. It's quite a bargain. Shipping and handling is just 50¢ per book in the U.S. and 75¢ per book in Canada.* I understand that accepting the 2 free books and gifts places me under no obligation to buy anything. I can always return a shipment and cancel at any time. Even if I never buy another book, the two free books and gifts are mine to keep forever.

151/351 HDN FEQE

Name	(PLEASE PRINT)

Address	Apt. #

City	State/Prov.	Zip/Postal Code

Signature (if under 18, a parent or guardian must sign)

Mail to the **Reader Service:**
IN U.S.A.: P.O. Box 1867, Buffalo, NY 14240-1867
IN CANADA: P.O. Box 609, Fort Erie, Ontario L2A 5X3

Not valid for current subscribers to Harlequin Blaze books.

Want to try two free books from another line?
Call 1-800-873-8635 or visit www.ReaderService.com.

* Terms and prices subject to change without notice. Prices do not include applicable taxes. Sales tax applicable in N.Y. Canadian residents will be charged applicable taxes. Offer not valid in Quebec. This offer is limited to one order per household. All orders subject to credit approval. Credit or debit balances in a customer's account(s) may be offset by any other outstanding balance owed by or to the customer. Please allow 4 to 6 weeks for delivery. Offer available while quantities last.

Your Privacy—The Reader Service is committed to protecting your privacy. Our Privacy Policy is available online at www.ReaderService.com or upon request from the Reader Service.

We make a portion of our mailing list available to reputable third parties that offer products we believe may interest you. If you prefer that we not exchange your name with third parties, or if you wish to clarify or modify your communication preferences, please visit us at www.ReaderService.com/consumerschoice or write to us at Reader Service Preference Service, P.O. Box 9062, Buffalo, NY 14269. Include your complete name and address.

Bestselling Blaze author Jo Leigh
delivers a sizzling *The Wrong Bed* story with

Lying in Bed

Ryan woke to the bed dipping. For a few seconds, his adrenaline spiked until he remembered where he was. He groaned at the bright red numbers on the clock. "One a.m.? What…?"

The rest of the question got lost in the dark, but it didn't matter, because Jeannie didn't answer. His fellow agent on this sting must be exhausted after arriving late. "You okay?"

She tugged sharply on the covers, pulling more of them to her side of the bed.

Ryan could just make out her head on the pillow, her back to him, hunched and tight. Must have gotten stuck at the airport….

He curled onto his side, hoping to find the dream she'd interrupted. It had been nice. Smelled nice. He sighed as he let himself slip deeper and deeper into sleep…. The scent came back, a little like the beach and jasmine, low-key and sexy—

His eyes flew open. His heart thudded as his pulse raced. No need to panic. That was Jeannie next to him. Who else would it be?

Undercover jitters. It happened. Not to him, but he'd heard tales. Moving slowly, Ryan twisted until he could see his bed partner.

He swallowed as his gaze went to the back of Jeannie's head. Was it the moonlight? Jeannie's blond hair looked darker. And

HBEXP1212JLREV

longer. He moved closer, took a deep breath.

"What the—" Ryan sat up so fast the whole bed shook. His hand flailed in his search for the light switch.

It wasn't Jeannie next to him. Jeannie smelled like baby powder and bananas. The woman next to him smelled exactly like…

She groaned, and as she turned over, he whispered, "No, no, no, no."

Special Agent Angie Wolf glared back at him with red-rimmed eyes.

"Jeannie is being held over in court," she snapped. "I'd rather not be here, but we don't have much choice if we want to salvage the operation."

She punched the pillow, looked once more in his direction and said, "Oh, and if you wake me before eight, I'll kill you with my bare hands," then pulled the covers over her head.

No way could Ryan pretend to be married to Angie Wolf. This operation was possible because Jeannie and he were buddies. Hell, he was pals with her husband and played with her kids.

Angie Wolf was another story. She was hot, for one thing. Hot as in smokin' hot. Tall, curvy and those legs…

God, just a few hours ago, he'd been laughing about the Intimate at Last brochure. Body work. Couples massages. *Delightful homeplay assignments.* How was this supposed to work now?

Ryan stared into the darkness. Angie Wolf was going to be his wife. For a week. Holy hell.

Pick up LYING IN BED by Jo Leigh.
On sale December 18, 2012, from Harlequin Blaze.

It all starts with a kiss

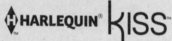